DEALBREAKER

GAMEBREAKERS #3

ELISE FABER

KAT MIZERA

GAMEBREAKERS

Icebreaker
Heartbreaker
Dealbreaker
Rulebreaker
Oathbreaker

ONE

Dash

"...AND THE WINNER IS... JADE CANTRELL!"

I knew she was going to win.

Her face is flushed with happiness and I'm happy for her—but something is wrong. I can feel it. I always do. I sense danger before it happens. So even though I smile and say all the right things, I'm on high alert.

So I see the guy moving toward the stage before anyone else.

Except I'm too far away to warn anyone.

Dammit.

My feet propel me in that direction but he's already on stage, moving toward Jade.

Yeah, over my dead body am I going to let him touch her.

I'm her bodyguard but she's also family.

"Jade!" I try to yell a warning but it's loud in here.

I pick up speed, pushing past two startled security guys who haven't yet figured out the guy on stage isn't supposed to be there.

Dumbasses.

Jade has moved away from the guy, but I'm finally on the stage.

"Get away from her," I growl.

"What are you gonna do about it?" The guy lunges at me, and I knock him back a few feet.

He comes at me again with a knife that I hadn't noticed before, and I side step him, but he's not giving up.

Little punk.

"Come at me, asshole," I snarl.

He grins and swings the knife around like an idiot.

But he's a dangerous idiot, and there are too many innocent people around to let this go on any longer.

"Put the knife down," I say.

"Fuck you!" He lunges again, and I wrap my arm around his throat, but I don't realize how close to the edge of the stage we are.

My left foot is in the air and then the two of us crash down a good five feet, hitting two tables and some chairs on the way.

I feel a sharp pain in my side and—

I JERK AWAKE, my heart beating wildly.

Fuck. Me.

How many times am I going to have the same stupid dream?

It's hard enough to get any sleep in the hospital, and these nightmares don't help.

It's been five days since the night the knife-wielding psycho fan tried to attack Jade, and it's all been a whirlwind.

One cross-country flight, thanks to Atlas, my controlling and overprotective billionaire best friend.

Surgery to replace the hip I fractured when I hit the table

on my way down, with the full weight of that idiot on top of me.

A boot to help the ankle I twisted when I landed.

And more MRIs and CT scans than I've ever had in my life to make sure there's no brain damage from the concussion I got in addition to everything else.

Brain damage.

Ha.

Four years of college hockey probably took care of that.

But everyone is determined to make sure I get the very best care.

I appreciate it. I do. It's just not easy for a man like me to be in a position where I have to ask for help. Ask if I can go to the bathroom by myself. Have a nurse give me a sponge bath. It's maddening.

I'm in a private wing of the hospital, because Atlas—along with my sister—insisted, and there are only a total of twelve rooms on this floor. All special cases with special medical needs.

It's irritating as fuck.

Two nurses move down the hall chattering away, like it's not two in the goddamn morning, and I let out a huff of frustration. I know they have a job to do, but is it too much to ask to give us—the patients—some peace and quiet so we can rest?

Apparently it is.

I sit up and reach for the walker I hate.

I'm supposed to be moving around as much as possible but I can't do it without the walker, and using a walker sucks. Between the new hip and the hit to the head, they don't want me to fall, and though it grates on both my nerves and my pride, I don't want to do anything that might keep me in this medical prison any longer than necessary.

I make my way to the bathroom and take care of business.

Then I carefully pull on a pair of sweats and a T-shirt. I slide my feet into the rubber-soled slippers my sister brought me, grab the damn walker, and take a tentative step. The hip feels pretty good, all things considered, but I still hate that I'm twenty-eight years old and had to have a fucking hip replacement.

I don't know if I'll ever be like I was before, and that's not acceptable.

Two tours in Iraq and I never got so much as a hangnail.

One night protecting country superstar Jade Cantrell—who happens to be engaged to my buddy Royal—and I might not be able to do what I do.

Fuck.

I clomp into the hallway, determined to wear myself out so maybe I can sleep for a few hours. I look left and right, trying to decide which way to go.

There are more rooms on the right since I'm one room from the end of the hallway, so I head in that direction. I feel like a decrepit old man, but at least I can walk. The orthopedic specialist that Atlas brought in told me once I heal and get through physical therapy, I'll be able to do anything I want.

Except—the more I do, the sooner I'll need to replace the hip again.

There's no cut and dried timeline, but if I run five miles every day, and push my body physically, I'll need another new hip in less than ten years. If I focus more on weight training and low-impact cardio, it could last me twice as long.

In my lifetime, I'll need at least two more.

I think that's the part I'm struggling with. Knowing that this hip isn't going to last forever. That I'll always have to be cognizant of my limitations.

I run an elite security and bodyguard firm that caters to the rich and famous—and they're not going to hire a guy with *limitations*.

There's no way to know what those limitations will be either, which bugs the shit out of me. At least, if I knew exactly what I'm dealing with, I could come up with a plan.

Instead, I'm wandering down a deserted hospital corridor in the middle of the night.

I'm almost to the other end of the hall when I hear voices coming from the last room. There shouldn't be visitors at this time of night, so I'm about to turn and head back in the other direction when I pick up a few words.

"...what game you're playing, but if I find out you're faking it, I will fucking end you. Do you hear me? You in there, Willow? You fucking stupid whore—there won't be any more of this fake coma shit when I get you home. And that's happening soon. So whatever you think you're doing, the jig is almost up."

The hair on the back of my neck stands up and I'm rooted in place.

Who is this guy and why is he talking to a patient like that?

I shouldn't get involved—it's not like I can do anything about it—but it feels wrong to leave. Instead, I duck into one of the computer alcoves the nurses use, my back turned.

A moment later, I feel him as he breezes past and I slowly turn my head, watching as the man practically saunters toward the elevators.

He's medium height, average weight, with curly dark hair and expensive shoes.

That's about all I can tell from the back.

Well, he has an expensive leather coat on too.

"Mr. Durand." One of the nurses I recognize—she's one of the nice ones—approaches him. "You know visiting hours ended a long time ago."

"I know, Holly, but I just..." He sighs, his tone so sad and emotional I wouldn't have believed this was the same guy if I hadn't heard him talking not two minutes ago. "...I hate that she's here alone. That she won't wake up. It's killing me."

"I know." The nurse puts a comforting hand on his arm.

"It's been almost a month," Mr. Durand continues. "Why isn't she waking up?"

"Head injuries are tricky. We really don't know. But the thing is..." Her voice turns serious. "If she doesn't wake up soon, they're going to suggest moving her to a long-term care facility."

"Absolutely not." He shakes his head. "I'm taking her home. I can take better care of her than any facility."

"She's lucky to have you," Holly says. "I'll see you soon."

"Good night, Holly." He gives her a blinding smile that almost gives me whiplash.

What the fuck is going on?

"Mr. Dash." Holly spots me and comes marching in my direction. "What are you doing out of bed?"

"It's loud," I say with a shrug. "How's anyone supposed to get any sleep? And I'm bored. And hungry."

She shakes her head. "If you go back to bed and rest, I'll defrost one of those acai bowls you like...with a little granola on top?" She wiggles her eyebrows playfully.

"Are you flirting with me?" I demand, trying to sound stern.

She's sixty if she's a day, and she giggles. "I am *not*. But I will if it means getting you into bed."

I laugh.

For the first time in a week.

And it feels good.

"Thanks for that," I say, smiling at her. "I haven't had much to laugh about this week."

"Part of my job... now come on. Let's get you settled and I'll find you a snack. You can flirt with me after you've gotten some rest."

We walk back toward my room, and my curiosity gets the best of me.

"Hey, Holly? Who's in the room at the end of the hall?"

Her eyes turn sad. "Oh...that's Willow St. Claire."

"Willow... oh, the *actress*."

"She had a bad fall, hit her head, and has been in a coma. They're not sure when or if she's going to wake up. It's such a tragedy."

"And that guy?"

"Her fiancé, Dylan Durand. You know, the big-time movie producer?"

I know the name.

Both names, actually.

Hell, you have to be living in a cave not to recognize their names.

They're a Hollywood power couple, and in my line of work, it pays to know who's who in the city of Angels.

And I intend to find out everything there is to know about Dylan Durand.

TWO

Willow

BEEP-BEEP. *Beep-beep. Beep-beep.*

The aggravating noise has been sitting on the edges of my consciousness all day, but try as I might, I haven't been able to part the fog that's sitting so heavily on my mind.

Beep-beep. Beep-beep. Beep-beep.

An alarm?

Am I late to set?

Or a fitting? Or—

Beep-beep. Beep-beep. Beep-beep.

To meet someone...?

Who'll be very upset if I'm late.

The beeping speeds up, the blackness surrounding my mind fading a little further.

Why would they be upset?

Why would that thought have panic clinging to the edges of my brain?

Why is everything so freaking foggy and confusing?

The frustration is enough that I finally hear more than just that godforsaken beeping. There's the rattling of a cart, the heavy whooshing sound of an industrial air conditioning system, and closer...

A voice that has the beeping speeding even further.

"...what game you're playing, but if I find out you're faking it, I will fucking end you."

Beep-beep. Beep-beep. Beep-beep.

"Do you hear me? You in there, Willow?"

Fingers grip my hand so tightly that I almost surface.

Only this time, instead of fighting my way toward the light on the other side of the darkness, I'm scrabbling against being pulled free of the fog, clinging to the shadows and the blackness, desperate to stay here.

Because *there* isn't safe.

This man isn't safe.

Thankfully, the thought has the shadows gathering again, dulling the pain in my hand, soothing the rough edges of my fear.

I still hear the rest of this man's words; the man whose voice wrought such fear.

But from a distance.

Because I'm sinking down again, safe and protected in that fog.

"You fucking stupid whore—there won't be any more of this fake coma shit when I get you home. And that's happening soon. So whatever you think you're doing, the jig is almost up."

I'm jostled, rattling the cage I've gathered around myself fiercely enough that I am almost propelled to the surface again.

Beep-beep. Beep-beep. Beep-beep.

But there are no more words.

And no more pain.

And...eventually no more fear.

At least until I sink even deeper into the shadows, until the memories crowd in and I remember why I've expended such effort trying to stay below the surface.

Away from reality.

Away from *him.*

"You're so lucky, Jade." The actress sighs and clasps her hand over her heart. "If I had a man like Dylan, I would—"

I can't let her finish that.

So, I do what I've gotten really good at over the last years. "Oh, I'm needed over there." I lean in and give her an air kiss. "So lovely to see you, Cara. Let's get together soon."

"I—"

I don't let her finish, just zip over to the other side of the room, stopping to chat with one of the catering staff.

We're hosting this party and it's been going perfectly.

A requirement because if it doesn't...

My arm twinges in memory of fingers gripping too tightly. My brain retreats from the recollection of Dylan's angry face, his cutting words.

That won't happen today.

There won't be any spilled platters tonight. No flat champagne. Not a single strand of hair or an eyelash out of place, no matter the tizzy I've worked myself into making sure all of that perfect is taking place.

No awkward conversations.

No smiles or inappropriate contact with members of the opposite sex.

Just Willow St. Claire and Dylan Durand—the perfect Hollywood couple—hosting a party where everyone is having a great time and totally, completely jealous of how in love we are.

It's all a façade.

But one that holds...

All the way until the last guest walks out the door and the caterers have been paid and tipped, the leftovers packed up.

All except for a plate for me and a single glass of now-flat champagne.

I'm ravenous because I haven't eaten since breakfast.

I've been too busy with all the party's last minute details and then hair, makeup, and getting myself into this dress to eat lunch.

And I was working the party—not all that dissimilar to how the caterers and waitstaff and bartenders had done. No, I wasn't hefting a tray or mixing drinks, but I was putting on that affectation of the perfect couple, sticking close to Dylan at the right times, disappearing as needed, so in tune with his needs and all the rest of the moving parts of the party that I feel like I haven't breathed all night. Instead, I played the perfect fiancée along with making introductions, ensuring conversations didn't grow awkward or boring, keeping an eye on the platters of food coming out from the kitchen, that the buffet set up along the far side of the room was constantly stocked, and making sure there was plenty of alcohol—always, there has to be plenty of alcohol—because this is how deals are made.

Or at least, how Dylan makes his deals.

Get someone a little drunk and they are far more likely to agree to the terms he wants.

Something I know.

Something I'm living.

Something I have no idea how to escape.

Because I haven't always been unhappy.

Once I thought he was my savior.

Now I'm worried he's my jailer.

Tonight, though, I'm too tired to be worried about the fact that the cage I've been living in seems to be growing smaller with each year that passes.

Will it eventually get so small that I can't breathe?

Can't move?

Can't—

"I told you that you can't eat that shit."

I jerk, nearly upend my plate of scavenged leftovers—two stuffed mushrooms, a couple of slivers of cheese, one piece of bruschetta, and a handful of carrots.

"You know that a pound on your frame"—Dylan's eyes drag down my body—"is ten on the screen."

"I'm hungry," I say quietly. "I haven't eaten all day."

His mouth presses flat, unhappiness in his eyes.

"And I have a session with Margie in the morning"—the personal trainer he hired—"I'll work out for an extra half hour tomorrow."

He releases his lips. "An extra hour."

God, that's torture.

But I don't argue.

I just nod. "All right."

The unhappiness leaves his eyes and the tension bleeds from his frame—and the room. I'm able to breathe a little easier, able to daintily chew on one of those mushrooms. Daintily because even though I want to shove it in my mouth, shove everything on my plate into my mouth, and then raid the pantry, I don't.

Dylan requires manners.

At all times.

I set the half-eaten mushroom down, reach for the champagne, mouth already watering at the anticipation of the crisp, fruity taste on my tongue.

But I don't so much as get the glass to my lips before it's swept out of my hand.

"No," he says.

"I—" My throat goes tight, nerves eating at my insides, but I *press on. "I'm working out the extra hour. The champagne isn't that many calories..."*

I trail off.

Because his face is changing again.

And the sinking feeling in my stomach almost has me hurling that half of mushroom right back up.

"You shouldn't drink," he says.

"I—" My throat is even tighter. "Why?" I manage to force out, and the flash of anger across his face has my throat loosening, the words coming quickly now. "I mean, I don't have to, and I won't. I promise, I won't. I just...you never seemed to mind before...and I'm just wondering why tonight..."

"Because it's not good for the baby," he says slowly, as though I'm the dumbest person on the planet.

And maybe I am.

Because those words don't compute.

"But I just had my—" I cut that off because he doesn't like to hear about my periods. "I mean, I'm not pregnant."

He slides his hand down my arm, taking my hand and drawing me to my feet, stepping close and pressing his body flush against mine.

He's hard.

I can feel his erection pressing against my belly.

I'm not turned on. In fact, I'm so not turned on that bile burns the back of my throat.

"You'll be pregnant soon enough and it's better to have good habits now."

Like not eating?

Like walking on eggshells so I don't set him off?

Like living in an ever-decreasing gilded cage?

Like...

No.

Just...

"No!"

The word blasts through my mind the same time it leaves my lips, the sudden horror and revulsion and terror over bringing a baby into this fucked-up situation erasing every bit of common sense I possess.

"What do you mean NO?" he asks coldly, his fingers tightening, his expression going scary.

I try to pull out of his hold.

But the move is far too late.

He's holding me. He's holding me far too tightly.

"Let me go," I whisper.

He doesn't. Instead, he grips tighter, pulls me closer, tone deadly when he says, "What the fuck do you mean NO?"

"Dylan," I begin, my hands covering his, trying to peel them free.

"I asked you a question, Willow."

I scramble, desperately trying to come up with something that will defuse this, something that will get this insane thought out of his head.

"I...well, we were talking about doing that film. It would be really hard to do pregnant or with a newborn or—"

"I'll adjust the schedule or we can get creative with shots and hiring help."

"I—"

"It's not up for discussion, Willow. You're having my baby."

I blink once. Then again. Then the only thing I can say is...

"No."

His fingers tighten. "No?"

I shake my head. "No, Dylan. I can't— I can't have a baby with you."

I haven't stood up to him in so long that the shock rippling across his face is abundant and it loosens his grip on me.

I jerk away from him, spinning on my heels, running for the hall.

I have nowhere to go, no one to trust, but I just know that I can't stay here.

Only I don't make it more than a couple of steps before a hand is wrapping around my arm, yanking me back.

He spins me around, his angry face in mine. "You fucking bitch." He shoves me and I stagger back a step. "You will do"—another shove and I teeter on the heels I haven't taken off yet, struggling to stay upright—"whatever the fuck—"another and I nearly go down, nails scrabbling at the edge of the counter to keep my feet—"I tell you to do!"

The last is a roar and accompanied by a push so hard that I don't have a hope in hell of staying on my feet.

I tumble backward.

It happens in slow motion.

I fall.

Not toward the floor.

But, off-balance, I topple toward the island...

Toward the sharp edge of the countertop.

I gasp, try to get my hand up.

Too late.

A crack.

A burst of pain through my temple.

And then the world goes black.

THREE

Dash

I TAP my fingers impatiently on the tray table as I peruse the papers in front of me.

A phone call to one of my cyber experts late last night resulted in having a file with all the information he could dig up on one Dylan Theodore Durand couriered to me here at the hospital.

Born and raised in Indianapolis.

Dropped out of UCLA his junior year because he got a small part in a big action-adventure movie. His acting career didn't take off but his producing did. And over the last ten years he's made quite a name for himself.

On paper, he seems like a great guy.

Handsome, wealthy, altruistic, and engaged to one of the most beautiful women in Hollywood. They're a power couple that everyone seems to love.

If I hadn't heard him talking to her with my own ears, I wouldn't believe that he was capable of anything nefarious.

Except there's a sealed juvie record my guy couldn't get his hands on.

Yet.

I told him it was a priority, and I didn't care whom he had to bribe to get a glimpse at it.

There was also an incident in college, but the details are sketchy, which bugs me.

A he said-she said situation where there was simply what's referred to as an "incident" in the report, and which was settled by the student services department.

Whatever that means.

That's a red flag if I ever heard one, but I know the woman's name, so I may send someone to talk to her. Something I would normally handle myself.

Except I'm still stuck in this fucking gilded cage.

My surgeon said I was good to go, but the neurologist said one more day of observation, since I'm still getting headaches if I don't take the meds. And it's a catch-22. Concussions can cause dizziness. Dizziness means I could fall. Falling could fuck up the already fucked-up hip. The same one I need to heal as quickly as possible.

So here I am.

It's one in the morning and I'm wide awake.

Again.

I close the file and shove it to the side as I get to my feet.

I'm more confident today, and though I still hate the damn walker, they said I can move to a cane if I don't have any setbacks between now and when I'm released. And since I'll be damned if I'll use a walker at home, I'm going to be careful.

Besides, I've walked past Willow's room multiple times today, making sure her dickhead of a fiancé isn't back. But she's been alone, which is as much of a relief as it is sad.

How does a beautiful, successful movie star not have a

single person sitting with her? Friends? Family? Private nurse? No one? Even the fiancé, who supposedly adores her, only comes by intermittently. The research I did tells me Willow has a very involved mother in her life...so where the hell is she?

It all feels a little off to me.

So I spend some time basically stalking her room.

She's as beautiful lying there in a coma as she is in the pictures I found of her online. In some ways, even more so. There's an innocence to her as she sleeps, and for some reason it breaks my heart that she might never wake up. I don't even know her but there's something incredibly... *vulnerable* about her as she lies there. It's almost like she's subconsciously asking for my help.

And I'm a sucker for a woman in trouble.

I hear a voice as I walk up to her room for the fourth or fifth time today, but this is a familiar one.

It's Holly, and I'm momentarily confused.

"*As no objection was made to the young people's engagement with their aunt, and all Mr. Collins's scruples of leaving Mr. and Mrs. Bennet for a single evening during his visit were most steadily resisted, the coach conveyed him and his five cousins at a suitable hour to Meryton...*"

What the hell am I listening to?

Holly must be reading to Willow.

Interesting.

Based on the verbiage, it's some sort of historical novel.

And for some reason, I'm rooted to the spot, listening.

Holly's voice is soothing, and the story gets my attention.

"*...Oh! No—it is not for me to be driven away by Mr. Darcy. If he wishes to avoid seeing me, he must go...*"

Mr. Darcy.

Wait, this sounds like Pride and Prejudice.

Briar made me sit through the movie once, but I fell asleep. Romance really isn't my thing.

"Mr. Dash, you should be in bed." Renita is one of the not-so-nice nurses. Well, she's okay, but a real stickler for the rules.

"I'm supposed to walk," I say calmly. "And I can't sleep. So the choice is either lie there and keep pushing the little button to bitch about anything and everything to the nurses or walk up and down the corridors without bothering anyone."

She purses her lips. "I'll give you fifteen minutes. Then I want you back in bed." She turns on her heel and disappears into a room down the hall.

"*...His behavior to myself has been scandalous; but I verily believe I could forgive him anything and everything, rather than his disappointing the hopes and disgracing the memory of his father...*"

The book is somehow much more interesting than the movie, and I stand there for what feels like a long time, listening to Holly read.

Sometime later—I've completely lost track of how long I've been standing here—Holly comes out.

"Mr. Dash." She smiles. "Lurking in the halls again? Do you want a sleeping pill?"

I shake my head. "No, thank you. Your voice caught my attention and then somehow I got pulled into the story."

"Pride and Prejudice. Such a classic. And apparently it's Ms. St. Claire's favorite book. Mr. Durand brought it in this morning, said maybe someone could read it to her. He heard that sometimes it helps coma patients if you read and talk to them."

"Yeah? So how come *he* isn't doing it?" I counter.

Her eyes meet mine, and I see a weird mixture of approval and disappointment in her eyes.

"I wish I knew," is all she says.

"So... does it?" I ask. "Help, I mean."

"We don't know for sure, but yes, there are stories from people who've come out of comas saying that they could hear loved ones talking to them. Reading. Playing their favorite music." She glances back to where Willow is still motionless on the bed. "But we're losing hope for Willow..."

"Maybe she just needs a little more time," I suggest quietly.

"We're hoping so." She pats my arm. "Anyway, I'm going to do my rounds and then come back and read to her some more. Try to get some rest, Mr. Dash."

"You can just call me Dash," I mumble. "Or Hudson."

"You look like a Hudson."

I don't think I know what a Hudson is supposed to look like, but she goes on her way and I pause in Willow's doorway, watching intently. I feel a little bit like a creeper, but I would never hurt her or do anything inappropriate.

I'm just worried about her.

I don't know her, and I don't know what's going on with her fiancé, but he scares me. There is no doubt in my mind he'll hurt her if he takes her home. Everything inside of me is screaming that she needs protection, and despite my injury, that's what I do.

I protect people.

People who are vulnerable in some way.

And Willow seems to be vulnerable in *every* way at the moment.

It's not like I'm going to fall asleep any time soon, so I look up and down the hallway, which is now deserted.

What would be the worst thing that could happen if I continue reading to her? Just for a little while. Maybe, if I'm lucky, it'll make me tired. If not, at least I can feel like I'm accomplishing something by keeping her company when she's spent far too much time alone.

I slowly walk into the room and sink into the chair at her bedside.

She's pale and blond, her slight figure hidden beneath what seems like a mountain of blankets. Eyelashes so light they're almost invisible as they dot her cheeks like lace, and delicate features make her seem doll-like. Her hair looks like spun silk, like someone has been taking good care of it since she's been in the coma.

Part of me wants to reach out and touch it, but I keep my hands to myself,

Instead, I reach for the copy of Pride and Prejudice. It's a hard cover, with fancy embossed leather and etched gold. The pages, however, are well worn and there's no doubt in my mind she's read this book many times.

I open to the page that's bookmarked and pick up where Holly left off.

"*'…I had not thought Mr. Darcy so bad as this—though I have never liked him. I had not thought so very ill of him—I had supposed him to be despising his fellow-creatures in general, but did not suspect him of descending to such malicious revenge, such injustice, such inhumanity as this…*'"

Elizabeth is not a fan of this Darcy dude. I may have to go back and read what I missed to find out why.

I chuckle to myself and keep reading.

At some point, I must have dozed off because I wake with a start, someone touching my arm.

"Hudson. Good morning," Holly murmurs. "It's six a.m. and time for your meds."

"Shit." I sit up and roll my neck. "I guess I fell asleep."

"A good book can do that to you." She takes it from my hands and puts it back on the table beside Willow. "Let's get you back to your room. I owe you a sponge bath today." She's kidding because I'm allowed to shower.

I groan anyway, just to mess with her. "I was just starting to like you..."

"You love me," she says, laughing. "Now, up you go."

For some reason, I'm reluctant to leave.

But I'll be back.

If for no other reason than I want to find out what happens next.

FOUR

Willow

"'...COLONEL *Fitzwilliam seemed really glad to see them; any thing was a welcome relief to him at Rosings; and Mrs. Collins's pretty friend had moreover caught his fancy very much. He now seated himself by her...*'"

There's a pause, a rustle, and I swim against the fog.

I love this story.

Love that even when everything goes wrong, it all still works out in the end.

"It's about damned time," that voice mutters, going off script in a way that tugs me close to the surface, tempts me toward consciousness. "Finally someone is getting their fucking head together and realizing what a gift Elizabeth is."

It's a male voice.

And that has my stomach churning, my mind freezing, panic and worry tangling with the present.

But pain doesn't come, and though the voice is gruff bordering on grumpy, it's not sharp at the edges, doesn't wound.

So, I stay near the surface and breathe evenly and...

Listen.

"'...*and [he] talked so agreeably of Kent and Hertfordshire, of travelling and staying at home, of new books and music, that Elizabeth had never been half so well entertained in that room before; and they conversed with so much spirit and flow, as to draw the attention of Lady Catherine herself, as well as of Mr. Darcy.*'"

He grunts, as though shifting positions because he's uncomfortable.

And, for the first time in what feels like forever, I notice that I'm achy and stiff and my nerves are on fire.

Like they're desperate to get to work and start moving this body.

"Yeah, now that some other dude is showing interest, you're going to pull your head out of your ass?" He snorts. "Douche bag."

I hear him shift again, the chair creaking, his grunt of pain audible, and I wonder if he's going to leave, going to stop giving me that gift of his voice, and I strain to move my hand, to reach out and stop him.

And when that doesn't work, I fight with my eyelids.

They're leaden and immovable, as though held in place by heavy weights.

And when the man with the gruff yet tender voice begins to read again, I give up the fight. I just do the only thing I can...

I listen.

"'*His eyes had been soon and repeatedly turned towards them with a look of curiosity; and that her ladyship after a while shared the feeling, was more openly acknowledged, for she did not scruple to call out. 'What is that you are saying, Fitzwilliam? What is it you are talking of? What are you telling Miss Bennet? Let me hear what it is.*'"

"Jesus," the man mutters. "She's a nosy bitch, isn't she?"

Then he goes back to reading, "'*We are speaking of music, Madam,' said he, when no longer able to avoid a reply.*'"

"Ugh," he grumbles and goes on, "'*Of music! Then pray speak aloud. It is of all subjects my delight. I must have my share in the conversation... There are few people in England, I suppose, who have more true enjoyment of music than myself, or a better natural taste. If I had ever learnt, I should have been a great proficient...*'"

"God," he mutters after Lady Catherine has continued to interject and dominate the conversation—and managed to insult Elizabeth's friend before walking away to bother the next person. "She's the worst."

I hear a soft thunk—the book being closed—and then a grunt that is definitely the man getting to his feet.

Not now, I want to tell him.

Not when Mr. Darcy is finally getting the courage up to approach her.

When they'll talk—well *she'll* talk—and tease—again, *she'll* tease. But the interaction will be the beginning of them.

Elizabeth softening.

Mr. Darcy falling in love.

Not when two of my favorite lines bookend a paragraph just down the page.

The first, "*You mean to frighten me, Mr. Darcy, by coming in all this state to hear me?*"

And the second, "*My courage always rises with every attempt to intimidate me.*"

If only that were true.

I hear rustling, footsteps.

"Goodnight, sleeping beauty," the man murmurs, and I feel the lightest touch on my hand, roughened fingers brushing against mine. "I hope your dreams are sweet."

I struggle against the fog, fight with my eyelids, my hand to reach out, to stop him from going.

Just a few more minutes, I would beg.

Just a few more minutes of the fantasy, of the happy ending, of everything that isn't my life.

And for a second, I win the fight.

Not with my eyelids.

But with my hand.

I feel it in the tip of my finger, the sensation rising to a peak...

And then it moves, rubbing against the coarse fabric of the sheet.

Only it's too late.

Because his hand is gone.

And I'm alone.

Again.

The next glimpse of consciousness isn't me rising up to hear the man with the gently rasping voice reading more of Elizabeth and Mr. Darcy's love story.

It's a conversation that's icy cold and filled with only sharp edges.

And it drives a stake of fear dead center into my heart.

Instinct has me diving deep, pulling that protective fog over me...

At least until the words belatedly process.

I freeze then, halfway between consciousness and nothingness, and I listen to the voices tangling with the steady beeping that seems to fill the room.

"...if she doesn't show improvement soon," a cool female

voice says, "we'll need to think about transferring her to a long term care facility. The hospital isn't where she needs to be—not now that her injuries have healed and there isn't lasting damage."

Hospital.

Of course.

I should have known.

The intermittent memories slide through my mind, one after the other. Hands poking and prodding, nurses and doctors talking to me.

Dylan's occasional visits.

A hand squeezing too hard. That frightening edge to his voice.

The threat always hanging in the air.

I've clung to the fog, knowing that I'm safe there.

Safe here.

And now?

"Lasting damage?" Dylan snaps. "She's been in a coma for weeks now. That's nothing if not *lasting*."

The doctor sighs. "I know it's not the news you want to hear, but we've done all we can for her here. Now the fight is up to her."

"That's bullshit."

"I have several great recommendations for facilities, and they'll be able to focus on what she needs when she wakes up—memory care, physical therapy, trauma counseling—"

"Trauma?" he snaps.

There's a long pause, and I'm not so deep as to miss the thread of disapproval in the air. "Waking from this type of condition often brings many complications."

"Well, be that as it may, I'm not dumping her in a facility." They're the right words, but the wrong tone.

Even in my fuzzy state, I recognize that.

The doctor seems to as well. "It wouldn't be dumping," she says cooly. "It would be getting your fiancée the care she needs in the place that's best suited to her recovery."

"The place," Dylan grits out, "that's best suited to her recovery isn't a rehab facility. It's our house."

"I don't think—"

The sharp edges of his words have softened, gentled, gone *charming*.

My stomach twists, the monitor's beeping speeds.

I know that tone, know the coaxing words will be impossible to resist.

I know because *I've* been cajoled and charmed and *coaxed* into staying, into giving, into bending when I should have gone, should have taken, should have stood straight.

"She'll be where she's most comfortable," he tells the doctor. "Surrounded by her belongings, by the scents and sounds of our home. She'll know she's safe and maybe that will help her come back to me." He sighs and I can practically picture the hangdog expression. The same one that's kept me tied to this man for far too long. "Because I need her to come back to me. I miss her so much."

The silence stretches.

Then the doctor sighs and my stomach begins to churn, the beeping on my monitor speeds again.

Because I know what that means.

There's tapping, as though she's dismissing the monitor's alarms. "It sounds as though she misses you too." The doctor's voice gentles. "Every time you talk, her pulse increases."

In fear.

In horror.

In desperation.

But I can't fight the fog enough to tell her that, can't make myself wake up.

Not even as she says, "I'll talk to the social worker, see what we can do about making that happen."

FIVE

Dash

"'*IN VAIN HAVE I STRUGGLED. It will not do. My feelings will no longer be repressed. You must allow me to tell you how ardently I admire and love you.*'"

I read the words and can't help but smile.

This is some seriously romantic shit. I've been reading to Willow on and off for two days and I can't put the damn book down. I don't know what's more interesting—the fact that I'm reading a romance novel or that I'm reading to a woman in a coma who I don't know.

Except I'm starting to feel like I *do* know her.

I've had my team dig up anything and everything they can find about her, going back to when she was a kid.

Overbearing stage mother.

Racy photoshoots and commercials starting at ten years old.

A wild streak in her teens, earning her quite the reputation.

Doing a movie with Dylan Durand that changed her career —and apparently, her life.

They moved in together as soon as the film wrapped and have been the couple about town ever since. Rich, beautiful, and the crème de la crème in Hollywood. They have it all on paper.

But I've started to find the chinks in the armor.

Bruises on her arm that makeup didn't quite cover up at a premiere.

The fact that she seemingly has no girlfriends—at least, none that I can find evidence of.

Cringe-worthy comments Durand has made in interviews that people have laughed off as sweet and romantic, when I find them controlling as fuck. I'm not a relationship kind of guy, but I would never talk about a woman I love like that.

I wish I knew more, but Durand keeps a tight rein on his private life, only allowing the public to see what he wants us to see. So much so even my guys couldn't get close to their palatial estate in Malibu.

Things are finally coming together in the book, and while I've become invested in the story, I'm a little bit more invested in what's going on with Willow and Dylan. He's not a good man. I didn't even try to hide that I was eavesdropping on his visit this morning, and the way he talks to Willow makes my skin crawl.

Insulting her, threatening, even roughly shaking her leg at one point.

That asshole is downright cruel.

It took a lot of self-control not to walk in and put my fist through his face.

A dozen times.

In my peripheral vision, I notice movement and I do a double take.

"'I think you are in very great danger of making him as much in love with you as ever.'"

Am I imagining that Willow's finger just moved?

I freeze, practically holding my breath, watching, and... there it is again.

Holy shit.

Maybe a few more pages will motivate her.

"'What made you so shy of me, when you first called, and afterwards dined here?'"

She stirs, shifting on the bed.

I've never seen her move before.

"Willow?" I speak quietly. "Are you awake, Sleeping Beauty? Can you open your eyes, honey?"

She's trying.

I'm no doctor but I can see it—see her—fighting the darkness, trying to make her way back to the light.

"You can do it," I encourage. "Just open your eyes for me, and I'll keep reading..." I don't know why I say that, but it seems to work because—

Jesus.

Cloudy blue eyes blink open.

Slowly.

She's *awake.*

Confused, sleepy, and a little out of it, but her eyes are open and now they seem focused on me. The tiniest frown appears between her brows, as if she's confused, and who can blame her? She doesn't know me from Adam.

I lightly put my hand on hers.

"Hey, there. Welcome back. You're in the hospital. You hit your head and have been in a coma for about a month, but everything is okay now."

Her thumb twitches, rubbing against the side of my pointer finger.

"Let me get a nurse—" I begin.

"N-nnn..." It's a hoarse, barely discernible whisper, but there's no doubt in my mind she's saying no.

"I'm not a doctor," I explain. "I'm just a volunteer...reading to you. You need—"

"P-plea..." She can't quite get the word out, but she's saying please.

Her heart rate just increased slightly—I can see it on the machine that's been monitoring her vitals—and the last thing I want is to upset her.

"Okay. Let's just sit here for a minute, so you can get your bearings. You want me to keep reading?"

There's a nod. Tiny but effective.

So I do.

"'*Lady Catherine's unjustifiable endeavors to separate us were the means of removing all my doubts...*'"

Man, this might be the most romantic stuff I've ever heard. No wonder she likes it. It's not my thing and yet I'm completely invested in the story and the characters. Not that I'll ever admit it to anyone.

"'*I am the happiest creature in the world. Perhaps other people have said so before, but not one with such justice...*'"

"Th-thank you," she says when I finish and there's a faint, faraway smile on her face.

"You're welcome." I close the book and put it down.

"Who...are... you?" Willow suddenly whispers.

"My name is Hudson. I broke my hip and got a concussion at work, so I'm a patient here too. I can't sleep at night, and thought reading to you might be helpful. But I really should tell someone you're awake. Your fiancé will be so happy to hear—" I say it as a test, to see how she reacts to mentioning Dylan, and the heart monitor immediately ticks up.

"N-no. Please. No." The soft blue eyes fill with tears. "D-don't."

"What can I do for you?" I ask gently. "Who can I call? Your mom?"

She shakes her head. "No. There's no one."

"Do you remember what happened?"

She closes her eyes again and sucks in a small, choppy breath before nodding.

I hate the fear that's practically emanating from her.

I've seen this kind of terror with dozens of clients over the years, but never with such visible vulnerability.

And this is exactly why I do what I do.

There's nothing I hate more than a bully, especially dangerous ones.

Like Dylan Durand.

There is no doubt in my mind he did this to her.

I close both my hands around her much smaller one. "Tell me what happened, Willow. You don't know me, but I promise, you can trust me. I heard him talking to you, so I know something bad happened. Or is going to happen. Talk to me. Let me help. Please."

She stares at me and I swear it's like looking into destiny.

I don't know what's happening, but there's more clarity in her eyes than I've seen in a lot of people who haven't been in a coma for a month.

As if she's weighing her options, sizing me up.

Then confusion mars her pretty face. "Who... are you... again?"

"My name is Hudson Dash," I repeat patiently. "I was in an accident and needed some specialized orthopedic care so I'm here at this hospital with you." I run down where we are specifically, and a few details about my surgery, hoping it will make her a little more comfortable. "I've had insomnia, so when I heard one of the nurses reading to you, I decided to take over."

"You know who... I am?"

I nod. "Yes."

"Is that why you want... to help me?" The fear and confusion in her eyes is gut-wrenching.

I wonder for maybe the hundredth time why someone like her is all alone.

And *scared.*

In the hospital.

With no one but a creepy fiancé who threatens her while she's sleeping.

It almost doesn't seem real.

But she's right in front of me, and Willow St. Claire is very real.

"Let me call a doctor," I say gently, reaching for the call button. "She can probably—"

She flinches. "No. Please. *Dylan* hired her. I've heard them talking..." She shudders slightly.

I release the button without depressing it. "It's the middle of the night. Chances are, your fancy specialist isn't going to come in, so it'll just be the on-call neurologist or whatever. Someone who can make sure you're going to be okay now that you've come out of the coma."

"You don't understand..." Her voice is more shaky now. "Once they find out I'm awake, he's going to lock me away at the house and—" She cuts off, closing her eyes. "You don't even know me. I don't know why I'm telling you this."

"I can help you. If you let me. *Trust me.*"

She gazes up at me, and I can practically see the wheels turning.

She doesn't know if she can trust me—how could she?—but she's terrified.

And it appears she has nowhere else to turn.

Her fingers absently twine with mine, squeezing with more

strength than I would have thought she'd have after being in a coma for over a month.

"He's...going to... kill me. But no one... believes me."

My chest squeezes painfully.

Over my dead body.

Bum hip or not, that's not going to happen.

"I believe you."

SIX

Willow

MY HEAD IS SPINNING, and it's hard to focus with the fatigue creeping back in.

It would be so easy to sink back down, to disappear into the fog and darkness, to never emerge again.

But there's a warm, gentle hand wrapped around mine.

Hudson Dash's hand.

His name swims out of that fog, reminding me why it makes sense that he might want to help me.

He's *Hudson Dash.*

Not a man who's famous and in the public eye.

But one who's known quietly within the circles of the rich and famous.

He runs a security company—or rather, *the* security company.

And he's just looked into my eyes and told me that he believes me.

My mom doesn't.

Neither does my agent.

The staff nod at me when I make requests, but don't abide by them until Dylan approves it. That goes for anything from the food I eat for breakfast to what clothes I want to wear to whether or not I have permission to get a massage or go for a drive or see my doctor.

Wouldn't want anyone seeing the bruises.

And any friends I might have once had have been lost to fame—jealousy that my career took back off when theirs didn't, toxicity because they couldn't kick the drugs we used to do until oblivion dragged us under, greed that my bank accounts were no longer accessible for them to drain.

They weren't accessible to them.

They *aren't* accessible to me.

"I don't know how I'll pay you," I whisper, staring down at his hand that's wrapped around mine. So much bigger than mine and marred with a myriad of scars. It's tan compared to the pale white of my skin, probably because he's allowed to spend as much time outside as he wants.

"I'm not worried about the money, Sleeping Beauty," he says quietly, and I lift my head, meeting the swirling gold and green and brown depths of his eyes. I love hazel eyes, love how every set is unique, love how they change depending on what their owner is wearing.

"I have money," I murmur. "I just...don't have access to it right now."

His gaze locks with mine and the air grows taut. "We'll get into why that is later. For now, let's focus on the best way to help you, yeah?"

His tone is...

I can't get a read on it—and that's terrifying because I've spent so much time and mental energy over the last years honing my abilities to do just that. Being hyperaware, searching for any avenue that would trigger the rage, tiptoeing around his moods.

"Are you mad?" I can't stop myself from asking.

His eyes flash and I shrink back into the mattress.

Definitely mad.

But his gentle hold on my hand doesn't change, doesn't tighten, doesn't *hurt* as he says, "Fuck, yeah, I'm mad. Real men don't scare women, don't isolate them, and they sure as fuck don't make it so they flinch away just because someone is pissed." He bends slightly, leaning closer, the golden swirls in his irises molten, his words growing even more intense. "And most importantly they don't ever—fucking *ever*—lay their hands on a woman."

The impact of those words...

Well, the beeping increasing on the monitor gives away how deeply they hit.

"You with me?" he says much more gently.

I inhale, forcing myself to do it steadily, easily. The beeping slows and I nod. "I'm with you."

"Good," he murmurs, fingers squeezing lightly around mine. "So, fill me in on the rest of it."

The memory of that night, the push, the pain, the *fear* that came when Dylan told me he wanted to have a baby.

No, that we were *going* to have a baby.

The beeping increases.

"Right." Hudson slips his hand from mine. "We can talk about that later. Let me grab my cell and call my team. We'll come up with a game plan and go from there, yeah?"

I nod. "Thank you," I whisper.

"In the meantime, let's get you checked out by the nurse and doctor—"

Beep-beep. Beep-beep. Beep-beep.

His eyes flick to the monitor and I watch a muscle flicker in his cheek.

Crap, I really need to get that thing turned off.

"I'll stay close while that happens," he promises, "and I won't let them do anything that you're not comfortable with or don't want."

They're just words, could easily be empty promises.

But...I believe him.

And maybe it's because I have no other choice *but* to believe him. Maybe I'm an idiot jumping from one bad situation and straight into another. Maybe this will all blow up in my face like so many other parts of my life have.

Maybe all of those are true.

More importantly, though, I know with absolute certainty that I can't stay here, can't keep going as I have with Dylan, can't go back to that gilded cage, that plush mansion that may as well be the world's worst prison.

I won't continue to be here on this planet if I do.

"Thank you," I whisper.

He nods. "Be right back once I grab the nurse." Those hazel eyes lock with mine. "I will be right outside the entire time, okay?"

Beep-beep. Beep-beep. Beep-beep.

I push down the nerves that creep in at the thought of him leaving.

He needs to make some arrangements. I need to get the clearance to leave, and we need to get those pieces in motion before Dylan comes back.

I exhale, the beeping slows, and I nod. "Okay."

"That's my girl," he murmurs.

Then he grunts softly as he pushes to his feet, and I see for the first time what he meant when he said he needed specialized orthopedic care.

His limp is intense.

And he's clearly in pain.

But there's pure grit in his expression as he uses the walker to move to the door.

"Hudson," I murmur, and he pauses, glances over his shoulder at me.

"Yeah, Sleeping Beauty?"

"I'm sorry you're hurt."

A flicker of emotion across his face, one I can't quite decipher, mostly because I'm still talking.

"But thank you for being willing to help me."

His mouth quirks up. "This is where I'd normally shrug and say, 'It's what I do.' But hobbling my butt around with a walker isn't *exactly* what I do."

I giggle softly. "No, I don't imagine it is."

Another flicker of emotion across his face, and this time the beeping echoing across the room isn't from fear.

It's for something else altogether.

"Be right back, princess."

"Okay," I whisper.

But I don't miss that he waits until my pulse on the heart monitor has completely stabilized before he slips into the hall.

The next half hour goes by at warp speed.

The nurse comes in and takes my vitals, and then I'm visited by a very nice female doctor who is *not* the woman that Dylan was speaking to during the worst of the conversations I remember, not the woman who was working with him to fuel my nightmares, who had me sinking deeper into the fog.

She's shrewd and calm and when Hudson hobbles back in and says that we're both getting discharged and "the fuck out of here *tonight*" she barely bats an eye.

Instead, she nods and tells us that she'll put the paperwork in.

It's all both fast and slow—the decision made, the moving parts in place. There's activity in my room and in the hall, where Hudson has been making quiet phone call after phone call, and there are long periods of quiet, where I'm stuck in the bed, just waiting.

I'm unhooked from the monitors, my stuff is packed up, and by the time Hudson comes back into the room and announces that our ride is here, I'm itching to get out of here.

Fatigue is creeping in.

I want to sleep for a thousand years.

But I can't let that happen.

Not yet.

Not until I'm safe.

So maybe that's why when he announces that our destination is his house, I don't freak out.

Maybe it's because he also pairs it with, "Right now, the best place I can protect you is at home with me."

Maybe I've lost my mind and I'm diving into the deep end.

Or maybe my instincts are telling me that for the first time in my life, I've found someone I can trust.

Either way, I just nod, climb into the wheelchair they've brought up for me, and say,

"Lead the way."

SEVEN

Dash

GETTING out of the hospital is epic.

Bringing Willow home with me... well, I'm not sure how I feel about that.

She's one of the most recognizable faces in Hollywood, and she's currently asleep in my guest room. My team arrived at six thirty this morning and we made it happen. Discharge papers for both of us, medical instructions, security issues... we needed to be out before Dylan arrived.

He was due at nine a.m., everything in place to bring her home, and thank fuck for nurse Holly. Once we got her on board, it was easy to get the information we needed to get Willow out of there safely.

I make a note in my phone to send Holly some kind of gift basket. We couldn't have pulled it off without her because Dylan was being very cloak and dagger about his plans. Luckily, I've been cloaking and daggering for a living for a lot longer than him.

Asshole.

Just thinking about him and the way he spoke to Willow makes me want to hit things. People. Probably just him.

What kind of prick talks to his fiancée the way he did?

Threatens her.

Promises to kill her if she doesn't do everything he expects.

I do a mental head shake to clear my thoughts as I stare into my refrigerator, trying to decide if I want anything to eat. I have a housekeeper who comes and freshens up, stocks the fridge, leaves meals in my freezer, and makes sure everything is running smoothly.

But she can't anticipate me being in a mood for I-just-spent-a-week-eating-hospital-food-and-want-something-different.

Maybe Willow is awake and is craving something special too.

I can order us something.

I'm not sure if I should bother her because getting her out of the hospital, into the limo, and settled in my guest room seemed to take a lot out of her and she was asleep by nine. It's almost noon now, so it might be a good time to check on her.

I take the stairs slowly—the doctor warned me to be careful for another two weeks—and stand outside her room for a moment.

This is my house, but Willow St. Claire is asleep... *right in there.*

After I snuck her out of the hospital.

It's a little surreal.

I knock quietly.

"Willow? You awake?"

"Come in." Her voice is soft but not overly raspy, so she may have been awake for a while.

Damn.

What if she needed something?

I open the door and step inside. "Hey, there."

The vision she makes lying there in the bed nearly takes my breath away.

Holly helped her shower last night, so her blond hair is down, tumbling around her shoulders in soft waves, and her blue eyes are clear and alert. Her skin is like porcelain, blemish-free and bright—definitely not like someone who just spent a month in a coma.

"Hi." She looks shy, almost timid, but she's sitting up, the copy of Pride and Prejudice I grabbed from the hospital in her lap.

"How are you feeling?"

"Pretty good, to be honest." She looks down. "This bed is very comfortable."

"My sister—Briar—picked it out, said guests needed to be comfortable. I told her that was the opposite of what I wanted because then they might stay longer. She laughed and called me an asshole."

For some reason, that makes Willow smile. "She sounds like a pistol."

I snort. "Wait until you meet my niece. Two peas in a pod. And Frankie just turned four. I won't survive the teenage years."

"I imagine that will be interesting." She looks around, as if taking note of her surroundings. "This room has a woman's touch. Your sister...or someone else?"

"The only woman in my life *is* my sister." I pause, realizing how that sounds. "Wait—I didn't mean it that way."

She laughs, and the sound is a delight. "No worries. I know what you meant. You and your sister are close."

"Our family is close," I say, leaning against the door jamb. "My buddies from college—Atlas, Banks, and Royal—and now Banks and Royal's girlfriends, Aspen and Jade. They're my family, along with Briar and my niece Frankie. We're together a lot. In fact, all the time. It's like having—"

"Do they come here?" she interrupts, a look of alarm on her face.

"Well, sure." I frown. "I mean, not often. We usually gather at Briar's house because she likes to entertain and it's easier for Frankie to have all her toys and stuff. But since my accident, I have a feeling they'll be checking on me a lot more often than normal."

"Oh, please, you can't let them see me." She sits up, shaking her head. "That's just too many people. Someone is bound to let it slip, and Dylan *will* find me. Don't underestimate him. Your family won't do it on purpose, but someone has a bestie who loves *Summer in Provence*, and they'll tell her I'm here and then...it will snowball. *Please*, Hudson. Promise me you won't say anything. Not until I've found an attorney and figured out a way out of this mess. Please." Her eyes fill with tears.

Christ.

I don't like keeping secrets from my family.

Especially not one this big.

And how the hell can I keep Briar from checking in on me?

But the look on Willow's face guts me.

She's in a panic, and I don't know how I can possibly make her understand the bond our family has. Briar and the others would never tell a soul, especially not if I explain the circumstances.

Of course, they're also going to have a field day with the idea that I have a woman I barely know sleeping in my guest room.

They'll get the wrong idea about it, and then it'll spiral into something I don't even want to think about.

Briar can be more diligent than the CIA if she thinks something is up.

Maybe it's in *both* our best interests if no one knows Willow is here.

Not yet anyway.

"All right," I say quietly. "I promise. But I don't know how long I can hold them off. Briar is bound to check in. And Atlas likes to stop by sometimes in the evening—we're both night owls—for a drink. If that happens, I can keep him downstairs, though. He wouldn't think to wander up here... as long as you're quiet."

"I don't have anyone to talk to but you," she points out. "I have no phone, no computer, nothing."

"I'm going to get you one of our burner phones," I tell her. "It won't be in your name, of course, so you can call anyone you like without them being able to track you. You can also create some fake social media accounts—I have tons of work-related emails you can use—so you can get online and see what's going on in the world."

"Oh." She looks startled. "Dylan doesn't like when I'm on social media so the only accounts I have are my official ones that my PR people run."

I stare for a moment, trying to understand how a woman like her allowed herself to be taken in by someone so controlling. I know it happens, but I never imagined it happened to rich, successful women too. I thought it was mostly women who didn't have money or options.

That's probably misogynistic, but at least I'm honest.

"Let me guess," she says when I don't respond. "You're wondering how I got myself into this mess."

I guess my poker face isn't working tonight.

"Maybe a little," I admit. "It just seems to me you could have left."

"And that's why no one believes me when I try to tell them who he really is." She sighs and leans back against the pillows.

"I do believe you, Willow," I say carefully. "If I didn't, you wouldn't be here. It's hard to wrap my head around it, I guess. I have so many damn questions."

"You can ask me anything you like," she says. "Though, I'm just not sure my answers will be very satisfying."

"And I'm not sure what that means."

"It means *I* don't even know exactly how it all happened," she whispers. "One minute, I was on top of the world, with a great new boyfriend who seemed to adore me. I had money, success, and even critical acclaim. And then slowly, one day, one step—one *shove*—at a time, it all disappeared. I can't even tell you when I went from happily in love to...terrified. That's how gradual it was."

"Is he the reason you hit your head?" I ask, trying to keep my temper in check. I'm not mad at her but all I can think about is Briar. If some guy did that to her...

"We argued," she says, her voice suddenly small and hollow. "He wouldn't let me have a glass of champagne, which was never an issue before. Then he casually announced it was time for us to have a baby—like it was a business deal or something. And that's when I knew I was in trouble. Because there was no way in hell I'd bring a child into my world. Not with him. So I told him I wasn't ready and he was pissed." She shudders suddenly, pulling the blankets up around her protectively.

"You don't have to talk about it if you don't want to," I say gently.

But she continues, her voice so flat it's hard to listen to.

"He was mad. *Really* mad. He told me I would do what he tells me to do, when he tells me to do it... then he shoved me and—that's all I remember. We were in the kitchen, so I probably hit my head on the edge of the island."

The roaring in my brain is like a freight train.

The vision of Dylan putting his hands on her—shoving someone as slight as she is—makes me want to hurt someone, hurt *him*.

"He'll never touch you again," I say in a gruff voice. "I can promise you that, Willow."

She slowly lifts her eyes to mine, and the look there is a cross between relief and doubt.

As if she can't quite allow herself to believe me.

But she can.

She *should*.

There's a reason I make a living protecting the rich and famous.

And there's someone who desperately needs my protection currently staying in my guest room.

Maybe it's because of my recent injury, or just because it's who I am, but I'm invested in this now. In her. And Dylan fucking Durand will have to go through me to get to Willow ever again.

EIGHT

Willow

"BITCH!"

I'm flinching back, trying to get out of arm's reach, but suddenly he's right there, his face a mere inch from mine...

Gasping, I sit upright, heart pounding, hand clamping to my chest.

Panic rippling through me, I search the room, and it takes a few moments to recognize that Dylan's not here, that I'm not in the hospital, that I'm in Hudson's house.

Safe.

For the moment, anyway.

That settles my pulse enough to reach for the burner phone—and that's a term I've never heard used outside of a movie script—and check the time.

It's after midnight.

"Dang," I whisper.

My sleep schedule is so messed up it's not even funny, and the fatigue that's clinging to my bones is even less so.

I know the doctor mentioned that it's common, that I spent a month in bed and my body needs time to recover, but I hate that I was exhausted by a ride in a wheelchair followed by a drive in a limo and a twenty foot walk into the house. I can't even count the flight of stairs up to the guest room, considering Hudson had one of his employees carry me up them and all but tuck me into bed.

I would have preferred Hudson be the one to do it.

And, good grief, just call me a spoiled princess.

Because of course he couldn't carry me—like literally *couldn't*—not with his hip.

And who am I to complain? I hadn't even been able to look at the steps without wanting to curl up on the floor and cry.

I should have been grateful for the lift.

I *am* grateful for it.

It's just...when Hudson touches me, I'm not scared, not holding myself carefully still, afraid to even breathe, so I don't trigger a ticking time bomb of a man.

Which sounds insane.

Because I've known him all of a day.

Except...he's *Hudson Dash.*

I know him by reputation, have never heard a whisper of violence or unwanted sexual advances, and this is Hollywood—rumors fly, we hear the rumblings.

But it's not just his reputation that settles over me like a warm blanket.

It's...an inner voice telling me he's safe.

"And what the hell do my inner voices know?" I whisper, setting the phone down and reclining back against the pillows. I pick up my worn copy of *Pride & Prejudice*, opening it and getting lost in the familiar words.

But as the pages go by, my hunger grows.

It begins as a slight ping at the edge of my consciousness then eventually becomes a gnawing ache.

I know the doctor told me to eat.

But it's the middle of the night and Hudson needs his rest, and...

He didn't say it was okay for me to go prowling around, rustling through his pantry.

So, I ignore my rumbling stomach and try to get lost in Elizabeth and Mr. Darcy.

Unfortunately, that only works for a few more pages.

Then I can't ignore my hunger.

It's grown so intense that I set my book down, toss the covers back, and slide out of bed. My legs shake a little bit as I slowly make my way out of the room and into the hall, but they calm down, my stride evening out as I descend to the first floor.

I'm almost feeling normal by the time I make it into the kitchen.

Aside from the ravenous beast demanding sustenance that's currently residing in my stomach.

On that note, I head straight for the fridge, intending to find some veggies and dip, something that won't go directly to my ass.

Only...then I see the chocolate cake.

It's mouth-watering, sitting there on the shelf, right at eye level.

I should have vegetables.

I *should.*

But I snag the chocolate cake from the fridge anyway, and when I see there's a slice already cut from it, I know my internal battle is lost.

I'm going to have cake.

Somehow, just thinking that feels like a huge step.

At least until I set the plastic container housing it on the counter and look up.

Then gasp and clamp my hand to my throat when I see Hudson standing there. "I'm sorry," I say quickly. "I-I'm just moving it so I can find some vegetables." A total lie, but his face is inscrutable and I can't see his eyes because he's standing in the shadows.

"You hungry?" he asks softly.

Mutely, I nod.

"And you're looking for vegetables to eat at"—he glances at his watch—"almost two in the morning?"

Another mute nod.

"Fuck that," he mutters, slowly moving forward, his hip seeming to be a bit stiffer than earlier as he walks to a cabinet and pulls out two plates and two glasses. Those, he sets next to the cake before he reaches for the knife block. "Grab the milk out and then close the fridge, yeah?"

I jerk, spin around, snag the milk, then carefully shut the fridge door.

By the time I'm turning back to face him, he's at the island, knife next to the plates and he's yanking off the plastic top that's sealing in the cake.

"Pour two glasses."

"Wh-what?"

"You allergic to milk?" he asks, setting the lid aside and reaching for the knife.

"No," I whisper.

"Lactose intolerant?"

I chew on the corner of my mouth then say again, "No."

"Then pour two glasses of milk, princess."

I blink once. Twice. Then manage to propel myself into motion.

I fill both glasses with milk then return the carton to the fridge.

"Forks are in the drawer next to the dishwasher," he says, cutting two huge slabs of cake. They're big enough that they'll give me far more than the proverbial ten pounds on camera.

I move to the drawer, open it, and snag two forks, then pause and tear two paper towels from the roll next to the sink. By the time I make it back to him, he's lifted both plates and brought them to the opposite side of the counter, pulling out a stool.

"Sit," he mutters, doing the same on his own stool. "Eat."

I hesitate.

But the cake looks amazing, and Hudson is already downing his slice and if he was mad at me for invading his kitchen, he wouldn't have cut me a piece and ordered me to eat.

I grab the glasses of milk and carry them over to our plates, sliding one toward him before I settle on the barstool.

"Thanks, princess," he says softly.

"Why do you keep calling me that?"

His gaze lifts to mine, holds. Then his mouth kicks up. "Because you looked like a princess sleeping so peacefully in that hospital bed—just waiting for your prince to wake you up."

My prince hadn't come.

Only my nightmare had.

Except...Hudson came to my bedside, reading to me softly as he roused me from my sleep, coaxed me to consciousness.

"Oh," I murmur quietly.

Then I slowly reach for my fork, heart skipping a beat as I scoop up a bite.

Part of me expects him to stop me. Another part—a bigger part—knows that won't happen.

I lift my fork to my mouth and eat that bite of cake.

Flavor explodes on my tongue, and I find myself cleaning

the tines of frosting and crumbs completely, trying to get every last morsel.

"You finish that," he whispers gruffly, "and want more—"

I hold my breath.

"—then you have another slice, yeah?"

"I shouldn't," I whisper.

"Life is too short to not eat cake."

"Why does that feel like the modern equivalent of Marie Antoinette saying *let them eat cake?*"

The words flow out of me in a rush, the sass something of my past.

Certainly not my present.

It's too damned risky.

But it slipped out, and Hudson is looking at me and—

Then he bursts out laughing and the tension is broken.

I giggle softly.

"You're funny, princess."

"Not usually."

Not anymore.

As though he heard that thought, his face softens. "Speaking of cake, want to hear a funny story?"

My heart skips a beat. "Absolutely."

And then he proceeds to tell me a story about him and his buddies, Royal, Atlas, and Colt, messing with another one of their friends, Banks, when he got it in his mind to bake a cake for his college girlfriend's birthday.

"Of course, he didn't"—his big chest rumbles with laughter —"realize we'd swapped the sugar for salt until they started eating it." He grins. "He never did close the deal—or make another cake, as far as I know."

I laugh. "You guys sound like menaces."

"You don't know the half of it."

"Will you—" I cut myself off, knowing I don't have any right to ask.

Soft fingers on my arm. "Will I what?"

I nibble at my bottom lip again then...go for it. "Will you tell me more about them?"

His expression gentles.

But then he does the most wonderful thing—

He starts telling me about his friends who are his family.

And I soak up every single word.

NINE

Dash

NORMALLY, I really enjoy my solitude.

I go to work, spend time with my friends and family, and then come home to peace and quiet. It's how I wind down, reflect on the day, and center myself. It's something I've done since leaving the military, and it's part of me.

I tend to resent any change to that routine.

And yet, I don't mind having Willow around.

In fact, I'm starting to crave her company. Sharing meals together—like our late-night snack—and just hearing her voice make me happy.

It's almost seven and I'm starving, but I don't want to eat without her, so I put the meatloaf in the oven and plan to wake her from her nap in a few minutes.

Instead, she surprises me; I was so lost in thought I didn't hear her coming down the stairs.

"Hudson?"

"Hey, princess." I turn with a smile.

Fuck, she takes my breath away.

"How are you? Ready for dinner?"

"Did you wait for me?" she asks in surprise. "It's late."

"It's always better to eat together instead of alone. Food's already in the oven. I hope you like meatloaf."

"I love it. Thank you." She gracefully sinks down on the large leather sectional and then stares at the TV. "Vipers are winning—yay! Go SoCal!"

That's another surprise. "I didn't take you for a hockey fan," I say.

She cocks her head, curiosity in her eyes. "Hollywood princesses can't like hockey?"

I chuckle. "Of course they can. I'm sorry, I shouldn't have jumped to that conclusion. You just don't seem like a hockey fan, but that's a bias on my part."

"Well, just so you know, I love hockey in general, but the Vipers are my team. I have three different jerseys, four T-shirts, more pucks than I can count, a couple of baseball caps, and Banks Christianson is my absolute favorite. He's *dreamy*."

She actually giggles, and a sharp twinge of jealousy catches me off-guard.

Banks is a good-looking bastard. Women love him. Almost as much as they loved Colt back in the day. I'm no slouch, but I don't compare to my enigmatic best friend.

"You know he's part of my family, right?" I ask quietly.

"Wait—the Banks you talked about is Banks *Christianson*?" Her eyes widen. "Oh my gosh! I somehow didn't put that together. I will totally fangirl if I ever meet him."

"His fiancée probably won't like that," I say dryly.

"I didn't say I want to sleep with him." She frowns, a flash of hurt in her eyes. "He's extremely attractive, but more than that he's an amazing hockey player. I mean, his stats have always been impressive and he's killing it this season..."

I open my mouth but then close it again. I need to stop being an ass. Thousands of women love Banks—as a hockey player. They're not in love with the man, just the fantasy he provides as a pro athlete. It's part of the job. There are probably hundreds of thousands of men who fantasize about Willow. It goes with the territory when you're a celebrity, whether you're an athlete or a rock star or an actor.

I know all of this, so I don't understand what the hell is wrong with me.

I don't *get* jealous.

Certainly not over a woman I barely know because she happens to be a Vipers fan.

"Yeah," I say after a moment. "He's always been amazing. We played together in college. I was nowhere near the player he was, though, which is why he went pro and I went into the military."

"You were in the military? You didn't mention that. Which branch?" She looks genuinely interested.

"Marines."

"Thank you for your service," she says quietly. "I don't get a chance to say that very often, but what you guys do—anyone who serves—is important. I never take it for granted."

"Thank you." I nod. "I would have played pro hockey if I was good enough, but it was obvious early on that it wasn't going to happen so I already had my Plan B in place. Colt and I both went into the military."

"Colt." She frowns. "Your friend...the one who passed away?"

We'd talked until five in the morning the night before last, and I forgot that I told her about him.

"Yeah." I sigh, always reluctant to talk about him to strangers. I'm not sure why either. He was a great guy. My friend—my *brother*—and one of the best people I've ever known. Deep down, I guess it's because I miss him but it's not easy to articulate that kind of vulnerability outside the family. "It's hard to talk about him. Losing him was...rough. Probably the hardest thing I've ever gone through."

"Then tell me more about the Vipers," she says, a smile on her pretty face. "Do you go to all the games?"

"Not all of them, but as many as I can. Recent hip replacement aside, I travel for work a lot, so I'm not always here. And we alternate staying home with Frankie if it's an evening game, because she can't stay awake that late."

"Makes sense—*yes*!" She lets out a yell as Magnus Forsberg sinks the puck into the net, giving the Vipers a three-goal lead.

"Fuck yeah!" I pump my fist. The guys are out of town tonight, so I wouldn't have been at the game regardless, but I enjoy watching them on TV almost as much as in person.

My phone rings, and I see Briar's name on the screen.

"My sister," I tell Willow. "I better grab it or she'll come looking for me." I tap at the screen. "Hey, sis."

"What a game!" she says enthusiastically.

"It is," I agree.

"I wish you'd come over to watch with us. Frankie will probably fall asleep soon and we could catch up."

"Catch up on what?" I ask. "I haven't left the house except to go to PT. There is literally nothing to catch up on." I glance at Willow, who playfully arches her brows.

"Did it ever occur to you I might have something to tell you?" she asks wryly.

"Do you?"

"No, but you didn't know that."

I laugh. "Seriously, I'm taking it easy physically, making sure the business is running smoothly while I'm out of commission, and doing my physical therapy. Everything here is cool."

"Frankie misses you."

That hits home because I love my niece. I love my sister, too, she's just a pain in the ass sometimes.

"I'll see her Sunday," I say. "I'll be there for dinner."

Briar sighs. "Okay. But you'll call if you need anything, right?"

"I'm fine, Briar. Really. Doc says I can drive in another week." I gentle my voice. Briar is a mother hen, and while it can be annoying, I know it comes from a place of love. We're family by blood *and* by choice.

"Don't rush it, okay? I want you to heal."

"I'm healing and doing what I'm told. Promise."

"I love you."

"I love you too." I disconnect and catch Willow watching me.

"I've always wanted a sister," she murmurs. "But my mother didn't want more kids."

"Briar and I have always been close. She was this tiny little red-haired angel when she was born and I loved being a big brother. Almost as much as I love being an uncle now."

"Being an only child means I'll never be an aunt," she says sadly.

"Don't you have girlfriends?" I ask. "Besties whose children would call you Aunt Willow?"

"Not anymore." She looks away. "Dylan isolated me from my friends. To be fair, I was pretty wild in my teens. That's kind of how this started. I rebelled against my mom and was partying like crazy. Alcohol, drugs, sex—I was living it up. That's when my mother took control of my money away from me."

"That's understandable," I say. "What I don't understand is why she gave control to Dylan."

"I think initially she was afraid I would start partying again. I was twenty-one when we met, and he was a calming force in my life. In the beginning, he was good for me. Older, settled, successful... just what I needed. Or at least, that's what I thought. Mom figured it would be a bridge to keep me grounded while I grew up. Her words, not mine."

"And your mom doesn't know he uses that money to control you?"

She rolls her eyes. "She thinks he's the greatest thing since sliced bread. It's ridiculous how much she loves him. I think Dylan gives her a stipend every month to keep her out of our business."

"He pays your mother to stay away from you?"

"I don't know for sure, I'm just guessing, but yes, I think so."

"There has to be something you can do."

"My mother got power of attorney when I was seventeen. It's still in effect. I don't know how to change it, and I don't have the money to hire an attorney to help me."

The oven's timer goes off, and I get to my feet. "We can talk about that over dinner, but that was the oven."

"Great. Let me help." She pads into the kitchen ahead of me and though I do my best not to stare at the sway of her ass, I honestly can't help myself.

She's a natural beauty. No makeup, hair in a ponytail, wearing one of my old robes—she still takes my breath away.

There's no universe where I'm anything but a gentleman, but fuck, she's making it hard.

Making *me* hard.

I've had a hard-on since she got here, and there isn't a damn thing I can do about it.

TEN

Willow

"DID YOU MAKE THIS?" I ask, taking a bite of the steaming food then promptly moaning.

Meatloaf, green beans, and mashed potatoes isn't a meal I eat often—heck, I can't think of the last time I've had such a stick to my ribs type of meal.

And it's delicious—the meat is tender and flavorful, the ketchup on top seasoned with something that makes me want to ask for more. The potatoes are buttery and smooth, melting in my mouth, and the green beans, well, they're green beans, but they're tasty, even if they are veggie-like.

"No," he says. "My housekeeper stocks my freezer." His mouth curves up just the slightest bit. "All I had to do was reheat it. Though," he mutters, and I notice he's pushed his veggies to the side, "I *can* cook things."

"Like what?" I ask, smiling as he makes a neat little pile of the green stuff instead of actually eating it.

"I can grill a mean steak."

My mouth tips up.

"What?"

"You can grill a mean steak?" My smile widens. "That's caveman for *Me hunt. Me kill.*"

He cracks up then leans across the table and tugs at a lock of my hair. "I can cook other things."

"Like what?" I ask again.

He scowls, but his eyes are dancing and I find myself teasing him.

I. Find. Myself. Teasing. Him.

I want to sit in that amazing fact..

But I don't want to be pulled from this moment, don't want to lose this light feeling inside me.

It's been too long.

"I'll amend," I say, "can you cook anything that doesn't involve slapping something on a grill and blasting it with fire?" I stifle my giggle as I scoop up another bite of mashed potatoes, making sure to get some of that tasty ketchup topping—call me weird, but it's delicious and I hope I get the chance to ask the housekeeper for the recipe.

Not that I can make it.

Or afford to hire someone to make it for me.

I could...try, I guess.

Try and fail.

Ugh.

"Hey," he says softly, "where'd you go?"

I exhale. "Nowhere."

"Liar." The accusation is quiet. Gentle. "Tell me." A little firmer, bordering on order.

"I can't cook," I whisper. "Can't hire someone to cook for me." I feel my throat getting tight. "Can't even go to the grocery store and buy ingredients to fumble my way through a meal." I push my plate back, close my eyes. "I just can't believe that I've allowed myself to get to this point."

"You know, I've been in this business a long time."

His voice isn't gentle, but I don't need gentle—don't want it.

That'll propel the tears over the edges of my eyes, sending them skating down my cheeks.

I'm so done with crying about my life.

I want to do *something*.

I suppose that's why I'm here.

Of course, it would be nice to actually have a plan on how to do that *something*.

"I've seen a lot of things, good and bad," he goes on, "but the one constant is that shit happens, it happens whether you follow the rules or not, whether you do all the right things or not, whether you're a good person or not. Hell, sometimes I think it happens more often to the good people because there's a line in the sand they're not willing to cross."

I think about all the lines that Dylan crossed.

And I shudder. "I just know that when it all gets out people are going to say *Why didn't she just leave?* Or *Why would she allow it to get to that point?* Or worse." I sigh, rub at the throb in my temple. I feel mostly normal, albeit tired with the occasional headache.

Though, I don't think this headache is from my injury and hospital stay.

It's because—

"I've asked those questions myself," I say. "Over and *over* again. I stand here and look back and feel like the weakest person on the planet. Because I don't have answers that make sense."

"Princess," he says, his big hand moving slowly across the table, gently wrapping it around mine. "We don't have to talk about this."

I don't want to talk about it.

And yet part of me *needs* to.

"You don't have to listen," I tell him. "I know you've been through your own injury and have your own problems." I try to slip my hand from his. "You're already doing enough for me—you don't need to be my therapist too."

His grip on my hand tightens, and I feel a sliver of worry slice through my middle.

Yet, even as I'm processing that, he immediately releases me.

Like he sensed that worry.

Like he *knew*.

I glance up into his golden-green eyes and *I* know.

He *knows*.

Deliberately, I shove down that blip of fear, concentrate on the things I *do* know.

He's kind.

He won't hurt me.

That's not something my heart or brain is telling me.

It's pure primal instinct.

Somewhere deep inside, my body knows that this man is safe for me.

"I'm a good listener," he says. "Because I don't mind doing it." A beat. "So long as you want to talk."

I take a breath, let it out.

It's not that I want to talk.

It's another *need*.

"I had an escape plan," I murmur. "Two years ago. I had money set aside, a plane scheduled to take me away from here. I thought..." I sigh. "I really thought I was going to get out. I was so careful—or I *thought* I was so careful. Then Dylan found out."

"How?"

"Our housecleaner. She found one of the bags I'd packed and told him, and then..."

"What happened?" His question is quiet...and full of rage.

But again, I'm not scared of this man.

"He shouted and yelled and"—I close my eyes, my hand convulsing around his—"it was the first time he got physical with me."

"Dammit," Hudson growls.

"I lost my allowance then. Couldn't so much as go out and grab a cup of coffee without him or one of his assistants glued to my side. Since then, I haven't made a move he hasn't known about—until you helped get me out of the hospital."

"Princess," he murmurs and I see the thread of anger in his eyes.

And the pity.

"Don't feel bad for me," I whisper. "I've done bad things, even though I had everything from the moment *Willow's World* premiered."

"Those teen shows are ripe with abuse, misbehavior, and vulnerable children."

Vulnerable.

Yes, I'd been that.

Vulnerable to drugs, to bad influences.

"Yes," I agree. "My mom was there, so deeply woven into my life I felt like I couldn't breathe, but they still managed to get to me. I was harassed by directors, told I would never measure up in any way by producers, given far too much freedom and access by co-stars. I drank by ten, got high within that same year, and my teen years were a mess. And the press ate it up." I rub the throb in my temple again. "Dylan helped me out of that. I was getting there—tired of using, of the partying, of waking up with people I didn't know in bed beside me, of looking in the mirror and seeing a facsimile of myself. He wanted me in his film and he took a chance and...in a way he saved me because he gave me a way out and kept me away from the bad influences until I was strong enough to handle them."

"A good thing." A beat. "At first."

"Yes."

I sigh, staring down at my hands.

"So, I guess the answer to all of the questions I know people are going to ask is that he saved me. And I was so scared of going back to that person I never wanted to be again that I didn't care how he did it."

ELEVEN

Dash

THERE'S a lot to unpack with Willow's situation.

We've talked a lot the last week or so, and while I have a better understanding of how it happened, I still struggle with her inability to walk away from Dylan.

Intellectually, I know her situation is complicated.

Her mother made a decision when she was seventeen that still impacts her today, and the fact that this incredibly wealthy, successful woman can't access her own money is mind-boggling.

I've put in a call to Madeline Aronson, an entertainment attorney who knows her way around contracts and litigation. Royal uses her, and she and Atlas are pretty tight, so I trust her, but she wants to meet with Willow and for some reason I've been loath to set it up.

It's ridiculous but we're in this private little bubble, just the two of us, and I know that I'll probably never have such intimate access to someone like Willow ever again. Once she leaves, she'll go on with her life, forget about me, and the truth is—I'm...attached.

Maybe that's the wrong word.

It's more like I'm invested.

In her, her situation, and our...friendship?

I've taken on a kind of protector role, but it's more than that.

We laugh a lot, working seamlessly in the kitchen as I teach her some of the basics of cooking and food preparation. She's a quick study, so it's been fun to spend that time together. Almost like a couple.

God knows, it's been a long time since I've been in a relationship.

College, actually.

Between being in the military, losing Colt, and then being active in Frankie's life, I haven't had the time or the inclination for relationships.

Willow being here has reminded me how lonely that can be.

Normally, I enjoy it.

Lately, not so much.

It's probably because Banks and Royal have fallen in love and brought two incredible women into our lives. We're a family, so anyone that's important to them becomes important to us.

Ironically, I'm breaking our unwritten family code by hiding Willow. This isn't how we do things, especially when someone is in trouble.

But I made Willow a promise and feel strongly about sticking to it.

There's an MMA fight on TV, so I'm in the kitchen gathering up what I need for an ice cream sundae, when I feel more than hear movement behind me.

"Hey, uh, Hudson?" Willow's voice is soft.

"Hey." I turn curiously.

She looks amazing in soft lavender sweatpants and a matching hoodie, her hair in a messy ponytail.

We did a little online shopping so she could wear something other than my robe and oversized T-shirts. She was extremely frugal, buying the most inexpensive items she could find, and using a notebook to keep track of every dime I spent. She's determined to pay me back, which is ridiculous considering how little it was.

"Is it okay if I make a sandwich?"

I frown.

"Willow." I can't keep the annoyance out of my voice. "I've told you a dozen times to make yourself at home. You don't have to ask permission. I'm not Dylan."

She recoils slightly, and I instantly regret my sharp tone, but this is the one thing that's gotten on my nerves. She asks my permission before she does almost anything. Eat, drink, watch TV—whatever it is, she comes to me first.

I understand she's a guest in the home of someone she barely knows, but I've told her it's fine. Anything she wants to do is okay with me. Hell, I'd let her sleep in my bed if she wanted to, though I didn't tell her that.

"I—I'm sorry." She dips her head, as if embarrassed, and I let out a huff of frustration.

I didn't mean to upset her, but she has to start learning that it's okay to be autonomous. That not everyone is like Dylan. That *I* absolutely am not like him.

I don't know if I scared her, hurt her feelings, or something else, but I need to smooth things over, so I put down the carton of ice cream in my hand and walk over to her.

"I didn't mean to snap," I say quietly, "but you've got to stop asking for permission. Contrary to the way you've been treated, you're not a child."

"I know. I just..." She pauses, her eyes fixating on all the things I've put on the counter. "Are you... are those... *sprinkles*?" She says it like it's a diamond or something.

"You like sprinkles, princess?"

"I haven't had sprinkles in... forever."

"I was about to make a hot fudge sundae. Do you want one?"

"I shouldn't." She chews her lip. "But I really do."

"Then make yourself one." I motion to everything that's laid out. "I only have vanilla ice cream, but there's everything else. Whipped cream, fudge, sprinkles, chopped walnuts, cherries—I can even slice up a banana if a banana split is more your style."

She stares at the items on the counter, a mischievous smile on her lips. "I want...everything."

I hand her a bowl and the ice cream scoop. "Have at it."

She looks at me for a moment and then puts the smallest, saddest scoop of ice cream I've ever seen in her bowl.

Oh, for fuck's sake.

I shake my head.

"Seriously? What the hell is that? A serving for a canary?" I pry the scoop from her hands and put two full clumps of ice cream in her bowl.

"Hudson!" She tries to protest, but I'm done with her being timid and shy and unsure. It's time for her to break out of the emotional prison she's been in and start living.

"Hush." I add a little of everything and then spray some of the canned whipped cream on the top. It splatters everywhere, little specks painting her hoodie and even her cheek.

"Hey!" Without hesitation, she flicks the whipped cream with her fingers, shooting a glob in my direction. It settles on the bottom of my T-shirt, and for a split second, we both freeze. She seems shocked that she did something so bold, and I have to resist the urge to laugh.

I look at the whipped cream, which is now sliding down my front, and then narrow my eyes.

"I see how it is... *this* is how you want to do things? Because I'll have you know I am a *master* at food fighting."

Her face goes from horrified to playful in a heartbeat.

She snatches the whipped cream can from my hand and squirts it full force onto my chest.

"Now it's on." I dig my fingers into the bowl of sprinkles and flick a handful in her direction, getting them in her hair, her clothes, and—my housekeeper is going to kill me—all over the floor.

"Don't come any closer!" she yells, holding out the can of whipped cream like a weapon. "I have whipped cream, and I'm not afraid to use it!"

I grab the nearby banana and hold it out. *"En garde!"*

We have a playful fencing match with our blades of choice, but then she gets close enough to squirt at me and she takes full advantage, catching me in the face.

Since I'm half-blind, I grab for the bowl of sprinkles and fling them in her general direction. She squeals, dancing out of reach around the island, intermittently shooting globs of whipped cream at me any time I get close.

I wipe the whipped cream out of my eyes and lick my lips. "Delicious—but you're still gonna get it!" I pick up a handful of vanilla ice cream, to the extent that I can, and take three long steps, wiping it in her hair.

"Eeek!" She screams with laughter, trying to wiggle away but I've trapped her between my body and the island.

Our bodies are close and for a moment everything stops.

I feel the heat, see her chest rising and falling, and it's hard to stop myself from touching her.

I stare down into her beautiful face, which is now rosy from laughter and exertion, and wonder how anyone could ever want to hurt this sweet, playful, and gorgeous woman?

Her lips part as she gazes up at me.

Fuck.

That's an invitation to kiss someone if I ever saw one.

But I'm conflicted.

I don't want to scare her off.

This is supposed to be her safe space. Where she doesn't have to worry about doing anything she doesn't want to do. Where no one hurts her.

And for the first time in my life, I'm not sure if I can—or should—make a move.

Before I can decide, the doorbell rings and I scowl in irritation.

"Fuck." I grab my phone and pull up the doorbell camera. "It's my sister."

"Shit." She backs away, grabbing a handful of paper towels and dabbing them in her hair.

"I'll get rid of her. Go on up to your room and try to stay quiet."

"O-okay." She looks panicked as she practically races out of the room and up the stairs.

Dammit, Briar.

I take a couple of seconds to get the worst of the whipped cream off my face and shirt, and then look around at the mess.

I'm going to have a hell of a time explaining this. I quickly stuff my bowl—the empty one—into the dishwasher and then head for the front door.

"Hey. What are you doing here?" I'm probably a lot less friendly than I should be with my sister.

"Uncle Dash! I missed you!" Frankie vaults herself in my direction, and I bend to pick her up before she can hit my legs. The hip is doing great, but I don't need anyone hitting me full force, even someone as small as she is.

"Hey, tater tot." I kiss her head. "What are you guys doing here?"

"We came to visit!" Frankie announces firmly.

"I just saw you on Sunday." I glance at Briar. "You could have called."

"You always tell me not to come," she says, breezing past me.

"You're sticky," Frankie says, wrinkling her nose as she wiggles to get down.

"I had a little whipped cream accident," I say.

"A *little* whipped cream accident?" Briar, of course, heads straight for the kitchen and she's now gaping at me, arms folded across her chest. "What the hell happened in here?"

TWELVE

Willow

I SWIPE AT MY HAIR, hearing the *clink clink clink* of sprinkles hitting the sink and counter and sigh, knowing I've made a huge mistake.

Hudson's kitchen...

Oh, it's a mess.

And he's going to be *mad*—

"No," I whisper, eyes flicking up to the mirror.

He'd be mad if I thought that.

If I believed that.

Because he's annoyed when I cower, when I ask if it's okay to eat something or go to bed or shower or wash my hair or... well, any of the things Dylan used to demand I ask permission for.

He doesn't get it.

I sigh again.

I guess I don't really get it either—even though I lived it.

How I let myself get ensnared so deeply. How I allowed myself to be made so small.

So pathetic.

I stare at my reflection, at my pale blue eyes, my blond hair. I'm objectively beautiful—something I know because I've seen my face blown up on a huge movie screen, large enough to dissect any flaws, to understand that mine add to the allure. It's something I know because I've seen the comments on social media, heard the red carpet interviewers dish about my body and face from the time I was a child.

A beauty.

Could be a model.

Are there people who think I'm hideous? Probably (no, *definitely*—something I also saw plenty of on social media). But they're trolls, people who live to tear others down.

I don't care what they think.

Because all I *do* care about is what Hudson thinks when he looks at me.

Does he see that beauty?

Or does he only look at me with pity, with sympathy, maybe even with derision?

I won the genetic lottery, but I definitely won't be winning any awards when it comes to growing a spine.

Pathetic teenage TV & movie star.

Pathetic adult—and I mean that strictly in the sense of being over eighteen—television & film star.

Sure, I have a pretty face and a great body...but I want him to see me for *me*.

"Ugh," I mutter, dropping my hands to the counter, dislodging more sprinkles in rapid *plinks* that hit the granite, the tile. "*I* don't even know who the hell I am, how can I possibly ask Hudson to see the real me?"

Unable to hold my gaze in the mirror—or witness the accusation in my own eyes—I focus on getting cleaned up.

I'm sticky, covered in whipped cream, the sprinkles he threw at me leaving little trails of color on my skin, my hair, my clothes.

Then, somehow, I find myself smiling.

His face when I tagged him with the whipped cream—

Shocked.

I'd braced, unable *not* to brace, but a second later his eyes lit up and the sprinkle attack began and...

I had fun.

Fun.

Something I'd forgotten existed.

Because my life has been work—working by learning my lines, working by training to be a ballerina or learning how to ride a horse or being taught how to handle a sword, *working* to be exactly what the director wants. And then working on the actual set during filming—being punctual, showing up clean-faced and ready for hair and makeup at my call time, those lines memorized and ready, giving something back to my co-stars during our scenes so we can create quality projects, being polite to the crew because they're the real heroes, taking critiques, focusing on the positives while promoting the project.

I love acting, even though sometimes it has felt like a millstone hanging heavy around my neck, a prison framed as a gilded cage as much as it is a way to live a thousand different lives.

But the craft, the process, the excitement of turning on the TV and seeing something I'm proud of, going to a premiere with my contemporaries and knowing when it's a good one, seeing it top the box office?

That's a high that's better than any drug I've ever taken.

Dylan gave me that.

The carrot *and* the stick.

I groan softly, wet a towel, and set to work on those tiny rainbows on my face and hair and clothes from the sprinkles, the sticky streaks on my hands and arms from the whipped cream.

Eventually, I realize I'm making more of a mess at the sink and slip into the shower.

Sprinkles on the floor, swirls of color going down the drain, tangling with suds from my shampoo.

But it's not until the loofa is trailing over my body that my mind drifts back to the kitchen...

God, that had been fun.

A mess and I don't love the prospect of having to dry my hair—there's enough of it that the going full finger-in-the-light-socket tresses by air drying is tempting—but by God...

It had been *fun*.

Hudson smiling as he launched sprinkles.

His laughter as I threatened him with my weapon of choice—that can of whipped cream.

He moved like someone who hasn't just had surgery.

He moved with power and grace and—

I *still* got him with the whipped cream.

My cheeks hurt and I lift a hand, realize that I'm smiling and must have been doing it for a while.

Something else that I almost forgot how to do.

A natural smile, not one carefully curated for the screen or for Dylan.

One that fades as I turn off the shower, snag a towel, and wrap it around me.

Because I'm back in another moment.

Hudson's big, strong body close, almost touching mine, his eyes filling with heat.

I wanted him to bend down, to close the distance between our mouths, to kiss me.

God, I had wanted that so much.

Then the doorbell rang.

Fate intervening, preventing me from doing something stupid.

But even as that thought is crossing my mind, my hand is lifting, pressing lightly to my lips, feeling the tingle there, remembering how much more intense the sensation had been when his mouth was mere inches from mine.

Remembering that the tingle hadn't just been in my mouth.

It had snaked down through my belly, trailed its fingers between my thighs.

What would I have done to chase that tingle?

Would I have lifted on tiptoe? Pressed my mouth to his?

Even as the questions cross my mind, I know I wouldn't have been that brave.

And I wouldn't have had to.

He would have.

And what would I have done with that?

Freaked out, panicking because the last time I kissed a man, it was Dylan and he's...well, *Dylan*.

Stilled before defaulting into actor mode—tilting my head for the best angle, unconsciously seeking out the camera, careful to keep my tongue in my mouth and my hands precisely in the places we agreed upon with the intimacy coordinator.

Or...

Would I have just enjoyed it?

Like I had enjoyed the last week, soaking in all that makes Hudson *Hudson*—his kindness and protective nature, his generosity and the capable way he handles his business, the love in his voice when he speaks of Briar and Frankie and the rest of his family.

I hope it's the latter.

Even as I know it would have likely been the first one.

"Ugh," I mutter as I shove the thoughts from my head and finish toweling off then squeeze the excess water from my hair. I pull out a pale blue dress I know I shouldn't have bought—it's unnecessary, impractical, and not even seasonally appropriate. But I bought two pairs of jeans, a multipack of sweatpants, a hoodie, socks, underwear, and shoes when Hudson handed me his phone, his Amazon app open on the screen...

And then I saw the dress.

In my favorite color—Cinderella blue.

Simple but with the barest hint of glitter along the hem of the skirt.

Something that Dylan would have never let me purchase, let alone wear.

Fun and young and pretty and innocent and—a version of me I've never been.

I couldn't resist.

I threw it in the cart, hit buy before I could talk myself out of it.

But after the way Hudson looked at me ten minutes ago in the kitchen, I want him to see me in this instead of the baggy sweats and hoodie I've been wearing around his house.

So, I don't overthink it. I put on the dress, tie the pretty sash around my waist, and turn around.

Then gasp.

Because there's an adorable little girl standing in my bedroom.

She waves and smiles. "Are you a princess?"

THIRTEEN

Dash

BRIAR IS ON A TEAR, determined to figure out why my kitchen is such a mess and what happened. If I let her think I fell and dropped everything, she won't give me a moment's peace. Nothing else will make sense, though, so I'm glad when I hear Frankie's footsteps tapping on the floor.

"Mommy!" Frankie's eyes are wide.

"You okay?" Briar looks up from where she's wiping down the counter—despite me asking her not to.

"There's a princess in the guest room!" Frankie announces triumphantly.

Jesus. Fucking. Christ.

I nearly groan but manage to keep my emotions in check.

"There's what?" Briar's brows knit together. "What are you talking about?"

"*Cinderella* is in the guest room."

If my life wasn't about to get hella complicated, I would have laughed at the excitement on Frankie's face.

Briar isn't stupid.

She also knows that Frankie is incredibly bright. She doesn't just make stuff up like this, so if she says there's someone in the guest room—even if she insists it's Cinderella—there has to be at least a modicum of truth to it.

Briar dries her hands and turns to leave the kitchen.

"Briar. Stop." My voice is low but firm. "I said *stop*."

She turns slowly, hands on her hips, the question in her eyes unmistakable. "Hudson?"

There's no way out of this.

She expects—and deserves—an explanation.

"I'm allowed to have guests," I say in an even tone that keeps Frankie from catching on to my frustration but gives Briar the clear indication that I'm not kidding around.

"Yes. You are." Briar seems confused. "But you've never hidden one before. Is this—oh shit." I don't know what conclusion she's come to, but it makes her glance down at Frankie worriedly.

"Briar, just let me—"

"Who's in the guest room?" Her eyes meet mine, hers filled with a combination of worry and curiosity.

"It's not—" I'm cut off by movement in the doorway.

"Hello. I'm Willow." And she breezes in like my sister and niece aren't about to lose their minds.

In a blue dress I've never seen before.

It's light and flowy, elegant, and probably the prettiest thing I've ever seen on a woman.

Or maybe she's just the prettiest woman I've ever been this close to.

Whatever it is, I'm momentarily incapable of thought. The most breathtaking woman in the world is just five feet away from me, and no one moves for a beat.

Frankie because she thinks it's literally Cinderella, and

Briar because there's no way she doesn't recognize Willow St. Claire.

"Holy..." Briar's voice trails, leaving her speechless for what's probably the first time in her life.

"I told you Cinderella was here!" Frankie snaps out of it and claps her hands in excitement.

"Please don't blame Hudson," Willow continues in a soft, friendly voice that shows no sign of her previous concern. "I asked him not to give me away. I'm trying to stay under the radar because..." She glances down at Frankie. "Well, I have some stuff going on in my personal life and Hudson has been kind enough to give me somewhere to lie low until I'm ready to go public."

"You were... I mean... when did..." Briar is sputtering, which would be hilarious under any other circumstances. My sister is rarely speechless. Nor does she sputter. She's the executive assistant to one of the toughest, most cutthroat businessmen in the world—Briar is always at the top of her game.

Except now.

"How about some ice cream, kiddo?" I ask Frankie since I can't think of anything else to say.

"Yes!" Frankie climbs up onto one of the stools next to the island, and I absently dump what's probably too much ice cream into a bowl.

"You should take that and watch some TV," Briar says, reaching for her daughter's hand.

"No. I'm good." Frankie grabs a spoon and takes a big bite of ice cream.

Yeah, she knows something is up and isn't about to leave the room.

The kid cracks me up sometimes.

If only this wasn't such a serious situation.

"I'm sorry about this," I whisper to Willow.

She gives me a quick nod and holds out her hand to Briar. "You must be Briar. I've heard so much about you."

"You have?" Briar cuts a dirty look in my direction. No doubt she's annoyed. "Unfortunately, I can't say the same."

"Again, that's on me. I've been trying to stay off the radar. I made Hudson promise."

Like anyone can make me do something I'm not willing to do.

And Briar knows that.

But right now, I think she's a bit starstruck.

"You... you're Willow St. Claire." Briar blinks a few times. "And you're staying with my brother. You were...in a coma... How did..." She shakes her head and then snaps her fingers. "You were in the hospital together."

"Yes." Willow seems more at ease than I thought she'd be, but if Frankie found her, what else can she do? I'm actually kind of impressed at how quickly she's adapted to this unexpected turn of events.

"The press is reporting that you're in some kind of rehab facility."

"*Dylan* is reporting that," I mutter.

Briar's eyes snap to mine and I can see the wheels turning.

"No one knows where I am," Willow reiterates quietly. Her gaze travels to Frankie, who's happily slurping up the last of her ice cream. "And it has to stay that way. For my safety—and for Hudson's."

I snort. "I'm not in danger from that punk. Bum hip or not, I'll snap him in half if he even looks at me wrong."

"Dash." Briar's voice is quiet but she looks over at Frankie, reminding me that she's in the room.

Like Frankie's never heard me talk that way before.

"Time for some TV," Briar says quickly, simultaneously

scooping Frankie up and wiping her face. "Uncle Dash and I have to have some grown-up talk with our new friend."

Frankie frowns, looking to Willow. "Can I call you Cinderella?"

"You can call me anything you like," Willow says lightheartedly, her eyes dancing with amusement.

"I'm sorry," I tell Willow when Briar and Frankie leave the kitchen.

"It's all right. She found me, so there was no point in pretending like she didn't see me. Now it's simply a matter of making sure they don't tell anyone."

"Don't worry. I'll take care of it."

"She's a baby," Willow whispers. "You have no way to control what she says—or to whom."

"She is and she's not," I say. "Frankie is incredibly mature for her age. Briar and I will figure out a way to explain it to her so she understands, without scaring her."

"Yeah, after you explain it to *me*," Briar says, joining us again. "From the beginning."

I give her an abbreviated version of events at the hospital, leading up to when Willow woke up.

"I knew I couldn't leave with Dylan," Willow says after a moment. "There's no doubt in my mind he'll find a way to kill me—and make it either look like an accident or like someone else did it. Well, after he gets what he wants."

"Which is what?" Briar asks in confusion.

"A baby." Willow shudders slightly.

Briar looks horrified. "What the fuck?"

"Yeah. I had a similar reaction." Willow shakes her head. "I'll die before I have his child. I'm not even kidding. I'm not suicidal, but I'd rather die than bring a child into his world."

"That's not going to happen," I say gently. "I can promise you that."

Briar rubs the bridge of her nose. "There has to be something we can do."

That's my sister—always ready to take action.

One of many things I love about her.

"Have you read what the media is saying?" Willow asks, looking a little dejected. "What Dylan has told them about me? That I woke up from the coma in an altered state. Distinct personality changes. Unable to care for myself. That he hopes rehab works... but that he'll remain by my side indefinitely, no matter how handicapped or incapacitated I am. He's laying the groundwork to declare me insane or have me institutionalized, or worse—make me a prisoner in my own home. Where no one can get to me."

"But why?" Briar looks mystified now, as if she can't quite wrap her head around any of this. It's the same feeling I've had —minus the anger that always brews just beneath the surface.

"I don't know," Willow admits. "It's a power thing, I guess. He knows that if he can't find a way to keep me against my will, I'll leave. And he can't bear the thought of losing. Not of losing *me*, but of losing whatever it is that he so desperately wants."

Briar makes a face. "He sounds... awful."

"You have no idea," I interject. "Which is why you can't tell anyone that she's here. I mean it, sis. It's not a game. And we have to find a way to keep Frankie quiet too."

Briar waves a hand. "She's the least of our worries. Lean into being Princess Cinderella and she won't remember that your name is Willow, much less your last name."

"We should talk to her anyway," I suggest quietly.

Briar nods. "We will. But my question to Willow is—how long can you hide out here? At some point, you have to start living your life again, you know?"

That's the million-dollar question.

And I'm pretty sure neither of us has an answer.

FOURTEEN

Willow

I DON'T THINK I've ever been more nervous for anything ever in my life.

Pulling into the driveway of a nice house in an equally nice, but nondescript neighborhood, seeing lights on in the windows, several other cars in the long driveway, parked along the curb in front...and my anxiety is ratcheted so high that my lungs are struggling to work.

Hudson puts the car into park and turns to me, hand slowly moving over the console, drifting toward me, eyes locked onto mine as though gauging my response to him touching me.

But I don't flinch away from him because he's safe.

He's kind.

He'll protect me.

I know that like I know exactly what Dylan would have done to me if I stayed.

Soft fingers brush over my cheek and my eyes slide closed for a moment.

Then I exhale quietly.

"It'll be okay," he murmurs.

Some part of me knows that too.

Briar and Frankie. Atlas and Royal and Jade. Aspen and Banks. He's talked about them enough that I feel like I know them already—and that time we spent together at Hudson's house a couple of days ago proved that Briar and Frankie are exactly as he painted them. But this is Sunday Dinner, the time where his family gets together, where they share good times, where they laugh and tease and bond and—

I've never had that.

Dinner parties where I play the perfect fiancée and hostess.

Drug-fueled benders where I drown out every worry about the past, present, and future.

Family dinners?

Absolutely not.

"You've won Frankie over," he says and my lids peel open to see him smiling gently. "You'll learn that she's the heart of the family. If she likes and trusts you, you're in."

Approval by a four-year-old is all it takes?

I find that highly doubtful.

And yet, I can't deny that Hudson's words loosen the knot in my belly.

"Good?" he asks, running his knuckles along my jaw.

"I'm good," I murmur.

"Good," he says, mouth tipping up.

Then he leans back, reaches for the handle, opens his door.

That unsticks me and I do the same, joining him at the front of his car and walking beside him up to the front door. His gait is so much better than even a couple of days ago, as though he never even had surgery in the first place.

Which is a good thing because we've barely cleared the top

step before the door whips open and Frankie runs out, launching herself into Hudson's arms.

He chuckles as he sweeps her up, settling her on his shoulders, and I can't help but smiling.

Especially, when I spy she's wearing a blue princess dress.

"Obsessed," I hear and turn to see Briar leaning against the door frame, her mouth tipped up.

"With her uncle?" I ask, and I can see why.

All that strong male energy going soft for a little girl in a princess dress?

Totally swoonworthy.

And it's not the first time I've thought of that when it comes to Hudson.

Something that...scares me.

But also...settles me.

"She loves her uncle, yes," Briar says, sweeping an arm to indicate I precede her inside. "But"—her voice drops—"she's truly obsessed with the princess in Dash's guest room."

I choke on a laugh.

"I swear I didn't mean to start that," I say.

"Four-year-olds gonna four-year-old." She tilts her head toward the kitchen.

"Oh," I say, remembering myself. I reach into my bag, pull out the bottle of wine. "I know it's not much," I whisper. "And it's not really mine. I insisted that Hudson bring it."

Her eyes sparkle. "Domesticating my brother. I like it."

"Who's talking about domesticating Dash?" I hear a male voice say.

I jump, heart twisting as nerves twine through my insides.

Briar's fingers brush over mine. "The broody man in a suit is Atlas." She lowers her voice. "The secret, though, is he's really a softie on the inside."

He scowls and shakes his head. "He's also your boss, Briar."

"Still not scary," she mock-whispers. "Mostly because he knows that if he makes me unhappy, Banks, Royal, and Dash will kick his butt."

Atlas scowls, but the beleaguered sigh he gives tells me that's true.

"Come on," Briar murmurs. "Let's open up this wine and relax while dinner is cooking."

"Is there anything I can do to help with that?"

Her mouth curves. "No, thanks though. Everything's just finishing up in the oven now."

"Plus," Hudson says, moving to my side and lightly touching my back. "Briar's a control freak in the kitchen. Better to just sit back and enjoy the wine you nagged me to bring." Light words and I look up, don't miss that he's assessing my face.

Whatever he sees there must be acceptable because he glances over at his family. "So, you've met Atlas. That grump" —a nod—"is Royal and the woman who somehow makes him smile is Jade—"

"Hey!" Royal snaps. "I'm not—"

Jade just pats him on the chest. "For what it's worth. I like you grumpy, honey."

God, his face—the way it goes soft and gentle for her—fills my soul. Albeit, that soft and sweet only lasts for a second because Hudson moves over to him and gives him a wet willy.

"Christ, Dash!" Royal growls, swatting him away.

Jade and Briar cackle.

Hudson dances away, grinning...

And ends up cornered by Atlas—and another man who I recognize as Banks.

Mostly because I've seen him on TV.

"You're Banks Christianson," I whisper, the awe evident in my voice.

He loops an arm around Hudson's throat, yanks him back against his chest.

My eyes go wide.

But only for a second because then I'm relaxing, my mouth turning up.

"Ew!" Hudson cries as Royal gives him a wet willy...in both ears.

"You know that payback is twofold, Dash," Banks says, releasing him and coming over to me. "I'm Banks and this is my fiancée, Aspen."

"Nice to meet you both," I whisper, feeling completely starstruck. "I watched your game the other night. Your goal was incredible."

He grins.

Probably because Hudson has looped an arm around my waist and drawn me against his side.

It's a lot of touching, and I'm unsure about the possessive nature of it, but I push that aside for now.

Because...it feels good.

"Thanks," he says as Aspen shakes my hand. "But it was a team effort."

A hand that's then filled with a wine glass.

Aspen grins, smoothing her palm over her pregnant belly. "Don't let him fool you," she teases. "He's on his best behavior the first time he meets you—"

Banks snorts.

"And by the time his ego slips out, you're in too deep."

"Rude," Banks mock grumbles.

"Deserved," Hudson mutters.

"Stop being grumpy, Dash," Briar orders, "and come over here and pull out this roast."

"Why do you guys call Hudson, Dash?"

Banks claps a hand on his shoulder as Dash releases me. "Because the man is as fast as lightning—or *was*."

I see a ripple of emotion slide across his—worry, frustration, fear, some combination of those three—but he turns away before I get more than a glimpse of it, going over to the oven and pulling out the pan.

I start to ask Banks more about the Vipers, but my question is interrupted by a tug on my hand.

"Princess Cinderella?" Frankie asks.

"Here it comes," Banks murmurs.

My brows drag together, wondering what those questions mean. I turn to face her, crouching down so we're at eye level. "Yeah, Frankie?"

"Wanna play Connect Four?"

FIFTEEN

Dash

SUNDAY DINNER IS ALWAYS a crap shoot as far as what's going to happen.

Usually, it centers around what Briar cooks and what Frankie wants to do. Sometimes it's games, other times she wants to show us what she's learned to play on the guitar or something she's made at school.

Once in a while, someone else gets to hold the reins, and we talk about Jade's upcoming tour or something to do with Banks and Aspen's baby. Hockey. Atlas's latest business deal.

Today, it's a mish mash. Frankie is inducting Willow into our family's Connect Four Hall of Fame—by annihilating her. It's particularly amusing because Willow has never played before. She never even heard of it, which breaks my heart a little. Frankie let her win the first game and then the gloves came off.

Luckily, Willow is a good sport.

Now that dinner's over and Frankie's immersed in her

millionth viewing of "Frozen," the ladies are in the kitchen doing whatever it is women do when they want an excuse to talk without us guys, and we're outside having a drink.

"Am I going to be the one who addresses the elephant in the room?" Royal says after a moment. "I mean absolutely no disrespect to the lady—but come on. Are you sleeping with Willow fucking St. Claire?"

I give him a dirty look. "Fuck all the way off."

"Dude, come on." Atlas cocks his head. "This is us. What's going on?"

"There's nothing going on!" I snap. "I'm helping her. That's it."

"Oh, *now* it makes sense." Banks' eyes twinkle. "You're upset because *nothing* is happening. You're into her."

"I'm not—" I cut myself off because what I was about to say feels idiotic.

Of course, I'm into her.

What living, breathing, red-blooded male who isn't already emotionally attached wouldn't be into Willow St. Claire?

"You're not...?" Royal makes a hurry up motion with his hand.

I scowl. "She's a client. She asked me for help. How inappropriate would it be if I made a move? Jesus, think with your big heads and not your little ones."

"But she likes you," Banks says, confusion on his face.

"You don't know that," I mutter.

"Are you worried about being rejected?" Atlas stares at me like he's never seen me before.

"Keep your voice down!" I snap. "Jesus, you guys are like teenagers sometimes."

Royal snorts with laughter. "More like horny teenagers, but sure. Whatever you say."

Willow's laughter filters out from inside and an unfamiliar

feeling of longing washes over me. I love the sound of her laugh and how relaxed she is with my family. Like she belongs.

Except she's not mine.

No matter how much I'm starting to want her.

I have to be cognizant of the fact that this is a stepping stone for her. Once we get her away from Dylan and she's able to access her money, she's going back to her world.

And I'll be left here in mine.

"It's a business arrangement," I say. "Yes, there were extenuating circumstances since I met her in the hospital, but she's scared and vulnerable. I would never take advantage of that."

The three of them don't say anything, merely watch me patiently.

Like they're waiting for me to continue.

I have no idea what they expect me to say.

"What?" I ask after a beat. "What the fuck are you fuckers doing?"

"Just trying to ascertain how long it's going to take you to get your head out of your ass," Atlas says, shrugging.

"It's obvious you like her," Royal says.

"And she likes you," Banks adds.

"We're friends," I say through gritted teeth. "And yes, of course I like her. What's not to like? She's obviously grateful that I'm helping her and—"

"Come on, man." Royal shakes his head impatiently. "What kind of bullshit are you spouting right now? If anyone recognizes that shit, it's me. I was spouting the same type of crap, trying to pretend I wasn't in love with Jade. I mean, why would she want a grumpy old sourpuss like me?"

"We're still trying to figure that out," I mutter.

"Shut up and listen." Royal points a finger at me. "Of all of us, you're the most closed off." He glances at Atlas. "Control freak boy over there is a close second, but at least he likes sex. You… you're like a monk in a cape."

Banks snorts, trying to hold back laughter, and Atlas is muttering something about not being controlling.

"Just because I don't flaunt it doesn't mean I don't have sex," I protest. "Not everyone is ready for the white picket fence."

"So you're going to sit there with a straight face and tell us if Willow flat-out said she was interested, you'd turn her down?"

Christ on a fucking cracker.

Why do they have to bust my balls like this?

I love them but sometimes they're a pain in my ass.

Well, a *lot* of the time.

"Look, it's not black and white like that."

"Then explain it." Royal looks annoyed and I don't know why.

I don't reply.

Not to worry, though, these fuckers have plenty to say.

"You spent a lot of time mourning Colt." Banks holds my gaze. "So you weren't in a good place emotionally. Then we were busy helping Briar with Frankie, which was a different kind of emotional crisis. *Then* you were completely immersed in getting your business off the ground, so you didn't have time. You also threw yourself into building the Sapphire Room, but at this point, I think you're out of excuses. I know I was."

"I don't have excuses. She's amazing. I just—" I cut off abruptly as Willow comes outside carrying a small tray with what's probably dessert.

Saved by the bell.

"Who's ready for something sweet?" she asks.

I have so many answers to that question, but none of them are appropriate.

She puts the tray down on the table and sinks into the spot next to me.

Right next to me.

So that her thigh is touching mine.

The spark of electricity between us is so strong I almost jump.

But her smile distracts me as she grabs one of the bowls and hands it to me. "Jade says it's her grandmother's banana pudding recipe. Dylan never let me have—" She cuts herself off and takes a breath.

There's an awkward momentary silence.

"Dylan never let you have dessert?" Atlas finally demands incredulously, his eyes narrowing. I gave him and the guys an overview of what's been going on when we first came outside, and don't miss Atlas growing more and more horrified with each new piece of information that comes out about Dylan fucking Durand.

He's not alone.

But his snapped-out question startles Willow, and she freezes for a moment.

I instinctively reach out to put a gentle hand on her leg, hopefully reminding her that she's safe here.

Thankfully, my touch seems to ground her, and I can't lie—I like that.

"No," she says softly, slowly reaching for one of the little bowls and a spoon. Then she gets a sparkle in her eyes that takes my breath away—strength and perseverance and...a hint of mischief. "But he's not here now, is he?"

And before any of us can say anything—she takes a bite.

Her eyes close and a faraway smile graces her features as she chews.

"Oh, my God. This is so, so good... it's just what I imagined."

"It's awesome, right?" Jade comes out holding a tray of coffee cups. She sets it down and passes them around before sinking onto Royal's lap.

The two of them are so damn...cute.

Disgusting, but cute.

And I suddenly have the strangest urge to pull Willow onto my lap, wrap my arms around her lithe body, and hold her. Let her know she's safe. Wanted. Part of the family.

Part. Of. The. Family.

My family.

The family I protect with my entire being.

The words ricochet through my psyche as I try to come to terms with that.

We don't invite people into the fold easily.

Hell, before Aspen, there had never been anyone.

The five of us—Colt, Atlas, Banks, Royal, and me—and then Briar. That's it. That's always been it. When Banks met Aspen and brought her to dinner, we knew immediately she would be part of the inner circle. The same with Jade.

And now it's happening with Willow.

Except it's different this time.

Willow and I aren't dating.

We're not even fucking, which is new for me.

Sex is usually all I'm good for when it comes to women.

It's been the opposite with Willow, and while I can tell myself it's because it's business— she needs me, she has nowhere else to go—I know better.

I could have put her in one of our safe houses.

I could have assigned one of my guys to take care of her.

I trust my team implicitly so there's absolutely no reason for her to be with me.

Unless—

I can't even wrap my head around words like feelings and... *love.*

Jesus.

I'm not in love—that would be ridiculous.

But there seems to be a serious case of the likes going on.

I like her.

She likes me.

We like spending time together.

My family likes her.

Frankie likes her.

Well, okay, Frankie adores her, but she's four. It's different.

But what the hell does it all mean?

My dick gets hard just thinking about her, so my dick likes her too.

"Hudson?" Her voice penetrates my racing thoughts.

"Yeah, babe?"

Shit!

Did I seriously just call her babe?!

I don't know if anyone else heard me, but she seems to take it in stride.

"You want to finish this? I'm really full from dinner." She's holding out a spoonful of pudding.

My mouth opens of its own volition.

But the sweet cream that touches my tongue isn't what I'm thinking about as I swallow.

No, I'm sitting here fantasizing about a woman I haven't even touched yet.

Yet.

As if it's a foregone conclusion.

Because I want it.

Want her.

More than I've wanted anything in a long time.

I don't know what the hell I'm going to do, because I think I'm... falling?

And I've never been more terrified in my life.

SIXTEEN

Willow

I'VE BEEN THINKING about the leftover banana pudding Jade tucked into my hands as we left Briar's house hours ago.

And when my stomach rumbled just after midnight, I gave in.

There's no one in this house who'll judge me for a midnight snack.

No one in this house who'll hurt me.

Hell, if Hudson hears me, he'll likely join me.

I tug my robe on over my simple pajama set of cotton shorts and a flowy tank, tie the sash and slip downstairs, not missing the sliver of light shining beneath Hudson's closed door as I go.

It's that bit of illumination that has me grabbing two spoons and the container of banana pudding. It's that soft glow that has me climbing the stairs and walking down the hall...then pausing outside Hudson's door.

I lift my hand to knock, but the moment my fist makes contact with the wood, the panel floats in.

Not completely closed I realize belatedly.

And that's the last thing I comprehend.

Because all my focus is on the bed.

Hudson is on the bed.

Hudson is *naked* on the bed and—

He groans, head dropping back onto the pillows, the chords of his neck standing out in sharp relief, his hips bucking, the squares of his ab muscles so defined as he strokes himself, it's almost like something out of a dirty magazine.

I'm awestruck.

I'm barely able to stay on my feet.

I want to be the one stroking. I want to trace the ridges of his abs. I want to kiss each and every muscle. I want—

"Christ, Willow," he rasps out, hand moving faster.

Christ.

Willow?

The banana pudding and spoons slip from my hand, the utensils clattering to the floor, the container dropping with a *thunk*, its lid popping off, the pudding landing with a *plop* on the hardwood.

Maybe later I'll mourn the loss of that delicious dessert.

Just...not in this moment.

Because the sight in front of me is so glorious that delicious midnight snacks are the last thing on my mind—or at least, delicious midnight snacks of the banana pudding variety.

Hudson is still, head lifted from the pillow, eyes wide as they lock onto mine. His hand is still wrapped around his thick, hard cock, paused mid-stroke.

Don't stop on my account, I want to say.

But, although I'm coming back to myself, or maybe finally beginning to understand the woman I want to become, I don't quite have the courage to go that far yet.

I can't stop staring, though.

And I can't make my feet move, can't find the strength to turn around and slip from the room, leaving him to his...private time.

And Hudson stares right back, eyes devouring me, dragging over the bare expanse of my legs, gliding up and I swear I feel phantom fingers parting the material of my robe, tracing between my thighs, over my belly, drifting along the hard buds of my nipples.

Then he seems to process what he's doing.

What *I'm* doing (which, for the record, is staring at his powerfully muscled body like it'll be even tastier than Jade's dessert).

He releases his dick, reaches for a pillow.

"Don't."

The word is torn out of me, raspy and guttural and so filled with need that my pussy throbs, moisture gathering between my legs, soaking the gusset of my shorts.

That same need finally has my feet unsticking—spinning around.

But I don't leave.

I close the door then spin back, watching his eyes flare at the soft *snick*.

He doesn't speak as I shore up my courage, give in to what I want.

What I *need*.

He said my name.

He—

I stop thinking, can't allow myself to think too deeply—otherwise, I'll lose every bit of courage I've managed to cobble together.

I sidestep the mess, take a breath, and approach the bed. It's only when I put one knee on the mattress that he seems to unstick.

"What are you doing, princess?" he murmurs as I straddle his thick thighs, his hands immediately settling on my hips.

They don't push me away.

They hold me steady.

My heart pulses, need mixing with affection—*holding me steady*.

Why do I feel as though he'll always do that?

Not hurting me. Not making me feel small. But, rather, supporting and bolstering and trusting in me and my decisions...even if they end up with a mess on the floor.

Then again, he doesn't seem to mind a mess.

Or cleaning one up.

Banana pudding. Sprinkles and whipped cream.

Po-*tay*-to. Po-*tah*-to.

"What am I doing?" I ask, smoothing a hand down his chest.

"Yeah, princess." His hands tighten slightly, and I shiver, the fabric of my robe parting.

His gaze drops to the triangle of flesh that's been revealed and heat fills my belly, spreads out from my center.

I want him to touch me there.

I want him to touch me *everywhere*.

"I'm finally taking something I want," I murmur, settling more heavily on top of him, feeling the hard length of his erection between my legs. I rock gently, pleasure spiking out from my center.

Too many layers of clothes between us.

But when I reach for the sash of my robe, warm fingers wrap around my wrist. "Princess," he murmurs, "look at me."

It's hard to focus.

My heart is pounding and my lungs are tight, and it's as though my skin has somehow become two sizes too small for my body. Am I really doing this? Am I going to do this with Hudson? Have I lost my mind?

What if he doesn't want it?

"D-do you not want to?" I whisper, cold water suddenly dumped over my head.

He said—

I assumed—

But maybe this isn't what he wants?

His face changes—heat warring with disbelief, humor with gentleness—and then he sits up carefully, abs doing wonderful things with the curl up, those sharp lines getting deeper, more impressive. He keeps his hands on my waist as he moves, drawing me back with him as he settles against the headboard.

"Baby," he murmurs. "You can feel my hard cock against that damp pussy—"

Heat floods through me—and it's not embarrassment.

It's need eating away at the worry, need ratcheting up the ache between my legs, need that has me rocking against him again, ever so slightly.

He grins. "Yeah, princess. You can feel that. So, you know I want to be inside you—"

More heat. More need. More desire.

"My only question is—" He waits until my eyes go back to his. "Is this what you want, Willow? Really, truly what you want?"

It would be easy to answer without hesitation.

To give in to the desire coursing through my veins and just say yes, just seek out this pleasure and not worry about any of the consequences.

But Hudson is a good man.

He deserves consideration.

Deserves to know that I'm not rushing into this without thinking.

That I want *him*, not just an orgasm.

So, I take that time, stop and consider all of what I'm feeling in this moment, and it's not until I've sat in my emotions and processed them that I cup his jaw, stare deeply into his eyes, and tell him...

"Yes, this is what I really want."

SEVENTEEN

Dash

THERE'S a good chance I'm dreaming.

I *have* to be dreaming.

There is no universe where Willow St. Claire is straddling my naked body, in my bed...

Except she is.

And I'm wide awake.

A thousand emotions rattle through me in this moment—the most beautiful woman in the world slipping out of her robe.

I watch as she tosses it aside but stop her before she can remove any more clothing.

You don't go from zero to sixty without a little...foreplay.

Hell, I haven't even kissed her.

But I'm about to.

"Slow down, baby." I reach up, gently caress her soft cheek with my fingers, and she leans into my touch.

She really is beautiful. Porcelain skin, delicate features, clear blue eyes, and lips I can't wait to taste. She's soft and vulnerable, but also stronger than anyone I know. She took a huge chance, leaving that hospital with a stranger, and now she's in my bed.

It annoys the fuck out of me that I can't just lift myself up and wrap my arms around her, but I'm supposed to be careful of my hip. I have the strength to do it, but everything is still healing, and if I wind up twisting the wrong way, I could dislocate it.

And that would be bad.

So I put both hands on either side of her face and gently coax her down.

Until our faces are close.

Close enough for me to feel the warmth of her breath.

"Are you going to kiss me, Hudson?" Her voice is like silk.

"Oh, yeah." I close the gap between us and the first touch is like dynamite. My cock is already on full alert, nestled between her still-clothed body, but even this small amount of contact is fantastic.

Our mouths move together slowly at first, feather-light kisses I want to savor. Her lips are just as sweet as I imagined and despite the growing ache in my groin, I'm in no hurry to rush things along. I also can't remember the last time I enjoyed kissing someone this much.

I nibble her lower lip, tugging a bit before I slide my tongue along the edge, making a little trail as I explore. Her mouth opens, inviting me in, and there's nothing delicate about the way she kisses. Our tongues do a heated dance, vying for dominance. She gives as good as she gets and we're kissing like we've done it a million times.

My hands travel along the curves of her frame—the indentation of her waist, the curve of her hips, and the shapely thighs currently straddling my torso. Even in the midst of our passion, I note how careful she is around my hip. Making sure not to put too much weight there, not rubbing too hard on that side... and I fall a little further under her spell.

I didn't think to ask the doctor about sex, but it's been five weeks—and there's no force on earth that will stop me from taking this as far as she wants it to go.

I pull away, because I can't kiss her and look at her at the same time, and right now I need both. The top she's wearing makes very little attempt at modesty, and I can see her nipples poking against the fabric. Her breasts aren't large, but they're perfect. Just like the rest of her.

I run my hands up across her flat stomach and slowly cup the soft globes in my hands. A quiet moan escapes her. I use the pads of my thumbs, rubbing them back and forth across her nipples, watching a soft pink flush work its way up her body.

"You like that, princess?"

"So much."

Her breath hitches when I squeeze her nipples between my thumbs and forefingers, just hard enough to get a reaction. As I suspected, she likes it gentler, and that's fine with me. I'm a big guy, so I never want a woman to feel overwhelmed by my touch —especially not Willow.

I'm enjoying the hell out of this new intimacy between us, feeling the ripple of soft muscle beneath even softer skin. Burning desire ripples through me as I struggle to stay in control—struggle to keep from ripping off her clothes and burying myself deep inside her. But something tells me that's how it always is for her, and our first time... well, *our* first time shouldn't be rushed.

Our *first* time.

Like it's a given there's going to be more.

"We need condoms," I manage to say. "In the bathroom."

"Oh." She looks startled for a moment but then smiles and eases off the bed.

"Under the sink!" I call to her retreating figure. Sure, I could get up and get them myself but watching her do it is more fun. The sway of her ass is delightful and—

"Did you find them?" I ask when she doesn't come out right away.

"I did." She stands in the doorway holding out a line of them that she lets hang from her hand.

But I'm not focused on the fact that she's holding about a dozen condoms.

I'm mesmerized because she's naked.

Willow St. Claire is fucking naked.

In my bedroom.

For me.

I swallow, my eyes glued to the magnificent woman who's currently taunting me.

"Jesus, baby...what are you doing all the way over there?"

"Waiting for an invitation." There it is—that hint of devilish humor that's starting to resurface more often. I love it.

"Come to bed, princess." I hold out a hand. It feels important that she comes to me, especially this first time. I have to be a million percent sure she's okay and feels safe and secure and... wanted. Hell, if she knows exactly how much I want her she might run anyway.

Thankfully, she sashays over to the bed, making a point of slowly dropping the group of foil packages on my chest. A laugh rumbles out of me, something I don't often do during sex, and she cocks her head slightly.

"I love the sound of your laugh," is all she says.

"I love the sound of yours as well." I trail my fingers along the outside of her thigh.

"Should I get on top?" she asks, pointedly looking at my hip. "Do you think that'll be easier for you?"

I hesitate. This isn't a normal pre-sex conversation, but

these aren't normal circumstances either. I like being in control, and love being in a position of power, but that doesn't seem important with Willow. In fact, my gut tells me I'm going to need to give over control for a while—until she's secure in... this. Us. *Me*.

"Yeah, probably." I take out a condom but she stops me.

"That's my job," she whispers, taking it from me and then straddling my knees. With her free hand, she wraps her fist around my cock and strokes up and down. Once, twice, squeezing harder, until I hiss out a breath.

"Too much?" she asks softly.

"No. It feels amazing." I watch in awe as she continues stroking me, her fist pumping up and down as if she doesn't have a care in the world. Except for the look in her eyes.

I love that it feels like I can see right into her soul. She's so raw and open and honest, and that arouses something in me I thought would never awaken. A beast I've kept tamped down tightly, unwilling to risk my heart.

Until now.

"Willow..." My voice is gruff, needy.

Without a word, she slides the condom down my aching shaft and then positions herself over me. Her eyes flutter closed as she begins to sink down, and I instinctively grab her hips, stopping her from going any further.

"Babe." It's a command and her eyes snap to mine.

"Look at me when I fuck you."

She shudders slightly, beautiful azure eyes filled with need.

And then she slips down. One. Fucking. Glorious. Inch. At. A. Time.

"Oh my god." The words are a cross between a gasp and a moan as I bottom out. "*Hudson*."

"Right here, baby. Keep looking at me." I thrust up, just a little, testing out how it feels on the new hip. I've done a lot in physical therapy but my cock lodged between this beautiful woman's legs wasn't part of any of *those* exercises.

This feels fine, though.

Well, it feels amazing, and also, the hip doesn't feel like it will give me any trouble.

"What do you like, princess?"

Her eyes pin me in place. "I like *you*, Hudson."

"I like you too." Sweat beads on my forehead, my control already beginning to erode. "But right now I need to know how to get you off."

"It's been so long since I had an orgasm, *I* don't even know."

We stare at each other and a million emotions run through my mind—rage at the asshole ex, need to break that streak...but it's a slender thread of humor that has me saying, "Then I guess the first one should be quick." I roll my hips up, and she settles more firmly against my groin.

"The...first?" She seems startled for a second.

"You didn't think there would be just one, did you?" I slide my hands up her sides, move across her breasts, and then tug her torso down as I stroke into her. "Kiss me, princess."

And she does.

Like a woman starved.

For affection.

For an orgasm.

For me.

I recognize her hunger because I'm starving too. I just never knew it was this particular woman I was hungry for.

She grinds against me as we kiss, her pussy clenching and fluttering.

She's already close.

And I am too.

"How does that feel, princess? You want harder, faster—?"

Suddenly she squeezes her eyes shut, her fingernails digging into my skin as her mouth falls open.

"Hudson! *There*—please...oh shit... don't stop!"

A tornado ripping through the house wouldn't have stopped me from finishing her off. I thrust and grunt, my balls tightening, instinct taking over. She screams my name, at least two or three more times, and it's the most beautiful sound in the world.

My woman, coming apart for me.

Her pussy milks my cock as I shatter, her body rocking over mine—the two of us completely intertwined. I don't know where I stop and she starts, and I don't care. She can take all of me. Anything. Everything.

Fuck.

I'm done for.

Unless and until she asks to leave, she's fucking mine.

EIGHTEEN

Willow

FOR ONCE, my dreams aren't filled with nightmares.

There's no Dylan hiding in the shadows, bursting out to terrorize me.

No scary memories of pain exploding in my middle, bruises and contusions carefully hidden by my clothes, my movements, no fists darting out to catch me unaware.

It's just peaceful oblivion.

And when I wake, it's gentle.

Because it's to the soft rumble of a male voice I know in my soul is safe, the same soft rumble that drew me out of the fog that had clung to my mind and kept me in the hospital, carefully ensconced away from Dylan.

My eyes peel back, and the fact that not for one second do I wonder where I am hits deep.

But in the best way.

I'm in Hudson's arms.

I'm safe.

And I'm listening to him talk, very quietly.

"...yeah, Atlas," he murmurs. "I'll let her know as soon as she wakes up. Thanks for the call."

My head bounces slightly as he shifts, setting the phone on the nightstand, and though I'm tempted to keep lying here in his warm embrace, the strong breadth of his chest beneath my cheek, the thrum of his heartbeat in my ear, his sigh is too troubled for me to ignore.

I lift up slightly. "What's the matter?"

He touches my cheek. "Promise me you won't be pissed at Atlas."

"I—" My eyebrows furrow, but before I can ask him what the hell that means, he shifts us, gathering me close as he reclines back against the headboard.

"Promise me that much, princess?"

My heart thuds hard against my rib cage. "Is he trying to hurt me?"

His eyes go wide. "God, no. Baby, he wouldn't do that. He got worried after what you shared last night and he did some investigating."

"Okaaay," I say carefully.

"Unfortunately..."

My heart thuds again.

"...that digging didn't take much effort—mostly because Dylan released a statement on social media today."

I suck in a breath, close my eyes, not releasing it until I know my voice will be steady. "What did it say?"

He gently tucks a strand of hair behind my ear. "I think it's better if you just read it for yourself." One hand settles on my hip, keeping me pressed to him as he reaches for his nightstand, snags his phone.

My heart...God, it's pounding so hard now that I can barely breathe, barely think, barely keep my body in this bed.

I want to run.

To allow that fog to slip over me and pretend my life isn't my life. To hide and cower and live a shell of an existence.

The urge is so strong that I actually feel my muscles tense.

But I'm not the woman who was with Dylan, the broken shell of myself.

I'm more.

I'm a woman who took a chance to make a better life for myself. I'm a woman who's learning to trust again even after the world has showed me its ugly underbelly. I'm Willow Fucking St. Claire, and that means *something*.

Maybe not much to the rest of the world who only sees me as Dylan's fiancée or the washed-up actress or the troubled child star.

But *I* know it.

Finally, I know it.

So, when he taps on the screen a few times and hands me the phone, I don't cower away from whatever curveball I'll be facing next.

I take the cell and force myself to remain calm as I read Dylan's post on Instagram.

WE ALL HAVE VARIOUS STRUGGLES AND CHALLENGES IN OUR LIVES, AND WILLOW IS NO EXCEPTION. WE'VE ALL SEEN HER BATTLE THE DEMONS INSIDE HER AND COME OUT VICTORIOUS. UNFORTUNATELY, THE WAR TO SOBRIETY ISN'T ALWAYS STRAIGHT.

IT'S AN UPHILL BATTLE WITH MANY VALLEYS AND SHEER CLIFFSIDES AND MUD-FILLED PUDDLES. THERE ARE MOUNTAIN LIONS AND RATTLESNAKES AND BLACK WIDOWS, ALL POISED IN THE SHADOWS, WAITING TO TAKE

A BITE OUT OF A BRIGHT, BEAUTIFUL WOMAN WHO I LOVE WITH ALL MY HEART.

AND RECENTLY, ONE OF THOSE PREDATORS HAS FINALLY PIERCED FLESH.

A FEW WEEKS AGO, WILLOW RELAPSED AND MADE THE BRAVE DECISION TO ENTER A REHABILITATION FACILITY IN ORDER TO GET BACK ON TRACK. PRODUCTION OF OUR NEXT FILM TOGETHER HAS BEEN PUSHED BACK TO ALLOW HER THIS TIME—

I GASP.

"I know, baby."

My eyes burn and I shake my head. "I know it's the least of my problems," I whisper, blinking rapidly. "But I was so excited to stretch myself with *A Whisper in Time.* Now, I'll be lucky to not be dropped from the film altogether."

"Princess," he murmurs, lightly stroking a hand along my side. "I'm so sorry."

I nod.

"We'll figure it out."

I'm not sure we will.

But I know that I haven't come this far not to at least fight for it—and if I still lose...

Well, I know I'll survive that too.

My eyes go back to the screen and I keep reading.

—AND WE LOOK FORWARD TO WELCOMING HER BACK WHEN SHE FEELS WELL ENOUGH TO WORK AGAIN.

IN THE MEANTIME, I'LL CONTINUE DOING WHAT I'VE ALWAYS DONE FOR THE WOMAN I LOVE: TAKING CARE OF HER, WATCHING OUT FOR HER, AND HOLDING DOWN

THE FORT UNTIL SHE CAN RETURN TO OUR HOUSE AND MAKE IT A HOME AGAIN.

PLEASE BE KIND, AND KNOW THAT ADDICTION IS A SERIOUS ILLNESS AND THE TRAUMA THAT CLINGS TO OUR YOUNG ACTORS IS A DIFFICULT MANTLE TO SHED. LET'S ALL SHOW WILLOW HOW MUCH WE LOVE HER AND SHOWER HER WITH LOVE AND SUPPORT AND COMPASSION INSTEAD OF DERISION AND HATE.

-D

"He's a fucking bullshit artist," Hudson growls.

"He's always been a great writer—probably why he's so popular." I sigh. "Too bad it's mostly a web of lies."

"Atlas is on the case," he says. "I have complete faith that he'll find a way to turn the right screws and get you back on the project. Plus, he's called Madeline Aronson and they're going to work together on this."

"The attorney?" I ask, mouth dropping open.

Madeline is famous in the business, no nonsense and smart.

He nods. "I phoned her a few weeks back to start looking into this, but her and Atlas working on this together means that things will move faster."

"And...she'll help me?"

Another nod. "If there's anything Madeline hates, it's when someone is being taken advantage of."

My eyes sting. "I don't know how I can ever repay you all for this."

"And I don't know how to convince you that none of us would be doing this if we didn't want to."

"It's too much."

"It's not."

I open my mouth to keep arguing, but he presses a finger to my lips, says gently, "So, Madeline and Atlas are on the case dealing with the conservatorship, and Royal got Kate Martensson involved—"

My eyes go wide.

Kate is like the best of the best when it comes to tricky publicity management.

And she has the waiting list to prove it.

"So, Kate is now on the case with that bullshit statement. And don't say he or Kate don't have to do that," Hudson adds in a hurry. "They want to help, and Royal's not going to stop until Dylan's curled up in the corner sobbing."

I smile at that image.

"Better," Hudson says, tracing the curve of my lips. "Now, I know you don't have access to your accounts right now, but Atlas said the conservatorship is supposed to deposit five thousand dollars a month into your account for incidentals—"

I set the phone on the mattress and shake my head. "*What?*"

He stills. "Can I take that to mean you didn't know about the deposits?"

"Dylan has never deposited money into an account I can access. I had a credit card that sent him an alert to approve every purchase, big and small, and sometimes he would give me cash. But I haven't had free access to any of my money—no matter the amount—not since my mom signed over the rights to him."

Hudson's big chest inflates then relaxes. "Okay, princess," he says. "That's not good exactly, but it sure as shit gives Atlas some ammunition."

Finally some good news.

"And hopefully we can use it to gain access to some of your

money so you don't have to feel like you're relying on me and can finally have your freedom."

I freeze.

Then my eyes start burning again.

Because...

This man is good. This man gets it.

This man won't shove me into a tiny box and put me up on a shelf.

"You're like my dad," I whisper.

His hand on my side tightens slightly. "Your dad, princess?"

"I-I—" My exhale is shaky. "I didn't know him because he died on 9/11 just a few months after I was born."

Hudson jerks. "Shit, baby."

"But you remind me of the man I created in my head growing up—the hero, the person who would climb a hundred flights of stairs to save people, who would put himself on the line because he valued the greater good over his personal safety. And he was kind and caring and he *loved* me." I close my eyes and a tear escapes. "Or at least, that's what the surviving man from his crew, Jim, told me."

Hudson wraps his arms tightly around me.

"The rest," I say, "I created, held in my head and heart, desperate to have someone who loved me for me."

"*Princess*," Hudson rasps. "Christ, baby."

"Jim gave me that," I say. "And he tried to stay connected to me, tried to be that dad while I was growing up. But when I was seven, he was diagnosed with cancer and it wasn't much later that he was gone. My mom...well, she took his loss hard, and I had far too much freedom for a young kid. It was pure dumb luck that I was spotted by a talent agent and not someone who truly wanted to harm me. Luckily, the agent was legit. Modeling came first. Then acting. Then...Hollywood."

He settles his forehead against mine. "Damn lucky, princess."

I nod. "I know." Then I sigh and straighten. "I can deal with Dylan taking the house and almost everything inside. I can deal with starting over and an empty bank account. But—" My throat is tight and I just barely manage to push the words out. "I just...before Jim died, he gave me a box with a memory book he made and some of my dad's belongings." Tears cling to my lashes and my words are watery as I remember Jim's handwritten stories, the medal issued to my dad, pictures, a trophy. The set of keys, a bottle of cologne, a sweatshirt that smells like my dad. Small things. *Invaluable* things. And most invaluable of all?

The only picture I have of my dad and me.

I dash away my tears, hold Hudson's gentle gaze.

"I can't let that box go. It's all I have of him."

NINETEEN

Dash

ALMOST SINCE THE BEGINNING, I've known what was eventually going to happen. That at some point I was going to have to confront Dylan. But I've been biding my time.

Technically, I've had no choice but to wait.

Partly because Willow needed to be ready, but also because I needed to be physically capable of handling things. Handling him. Yes, my team—they're top-notch—is capable of taking care of just about anything without input from me. But this is personal. This is about my woman, not some faceless client.

I'm doing well. I'm young, strong, and otherwise healthy, so the hip is healing in record time. Despite that, it's not a hundred percent yet. There's nothing that will get me there other than time, and it's only been six weeks. I can drive, work out—make love to my girl in the shower, on the bed, and against the wall—and do almost everything else.

But get into an unplanned physical altercation outside of the gym?

The doctor strongly recommended that I don't do anything like that for at least three months. Six if I want to be safe and really give the hip time to heal. He understands what I do for a living, but I have to acknowledge my limitations. Something I've never had to do before.

And it pisses me off.

Especially now.

Willow wants and needs certain things from the house. They're hers, and even if everything Dylan is saying about her was true, she still has the right to personal mementos and underwear.

So we're going to get them.

I know it's dangerous, and it pisses me off more than I'd like to admit, but this is our only alternative since her dad's things mean so much to her. Besides, I know if Colt was here he'd kick my ass for even hesitating.

Some days, I miss him more than others.

Today, I long for his counsel. His warped sense of humor. And the deep, dark code of honor he lived by. There was no one more determined to right a wrong, protect the innocent, and take care of those in need.

But he's gone, and I have to keep going.

Willow needs me so there's no time to reminisce with the ghost of Colt Blackwood.

I reach out to the two guys on my team I trust the most, Chuck Banner and Tyrone Clayton, to accompany us. Tyrone was in the military with Colt and me, and Chuck is my second in command at the company. He took over when I was hurt and handled things until I was back on my feet.

It's imperative to not only bring back-up in case things go sideways, but also that they be trustworthy because Willow is nervous. Since she can't be sure what Dylan's schedule is, we're winging it.

She believes late morning is the safest time to go to the house because historically he's most likely not there. He gets up, works out, and then meets up with friends or clients until sometime in the afternoon.

We can't know for sure that's what he's doing today, but there's no time like the present.

There are codes to get in the front gate and the doors of the house, and Willow feels confident they haven't been changed.

We pull up to the sprawling Beverly Hills estate and I punch in the code she gave me, since I'm driving. Willow's in the back seat with Ty, and Chuck is next to me.

"He usually leaves his Porsche in the circular driveway," Willow says, her voice tight as the gate swings open.

I glance in the rearview mirror. "Relax, babe. Everything is going to be fine."

I pull to a stop near the front door and turn off the engine, grateful there's no Porsche in sight.

"Remember—stay with me. Just lead the way to get your things. Ty and Chuck will handle anything that comes up."

She swallows, her face pale, but she nods.

She has a death grip on my hand when I help her out of the car. I note that her hand shakes a little as she punches in another code but visibly relaxes when the lock disengages.

Dylan will probably get some sort of alert that someone is at the house and see Willow, so it goes without saying that we have to hurry.

"Ms. Willow?" A stern-looking older woman comes around the corner, a duster in her hand, and frowns.

"Mrs. Wilkes." Willow nods at her. "I'm here to get some of my things. Excuse us." She steps around her and almost runs up one side of the divided stairway.

The house, with the ten seconds I have to study it, is beautiful if not somewhat sterile. Everything is expensive but bland—like someone with more money than taste decorated it.

"This is... the master bedroom." She throws open a set of double doors and heads for a row of bookshelves lining one wall. She touches a hidden button and a panel swings open—into the biggest closet I've ever seen. And I have a lot of rich clients.

But this is something else.

Floor-to-ceiling rows of shoes and purses, a line of suits that goes farther than the eye can see, and hangers of shirts and dresses in every color of the rainbow.

Yet Willow doesn't seem to notice. She immediately goes to the far corner and moves a row of luggage around, looking for a specific piece. She lays the largest bag down, opens it, and makes a soft noise of distress.

"What's wrong?"

"He moved it. The bastard moved it!" She hurriedly begins opening all the luggage. Some have smaller pieces of luggage inside them, and she opens those too.

"Damn him!" She looks up at me with tears in her eyes.

"Don't panic," I say in a firm voice. "Think. Where else could it be?"

She chews her lower lip.

Then her eyes widen.

She walks over to what looks like Dylan's side of the closet, pushing aside a portion of the suits. There's a shelf behind it, along with office style boxes, and she starts opening them.

At the very back, she pulls the cover off one last box, and inside is a smaller, nondescript box and she clutches it to her chest.

"Is that it?" I ask.

She nods, visibly relieved.

"Do you want to get anything else? We're here... so, if you

have underwear or jeans or anything else that might make you more comfortable, this is your chance."

She looks conflicted but nods. "I could use a few things."

Mrs. Wilkes walks in, arms folded. "Mr. Durand has very specific orders about you not taking anything out of this house. I've alerted security."

"These are my father's things," Willow says. "And if you think—"

"Babe." I touch her arm. "Don't waste time. Get what you need so we can go."

She grabs half a dozen neatly folded pairs of jeans, along with some shirts, under things, and a couple pairs of shoes.

"Boss." Ty nudges me. "He's here."

"Out of time, babe," I murmur to Willow.

She zips the suitcase closed and stands up.

"I got it," Chuck says, grabbing the handle.

Mrs. Wilkes has been watching us like a hawk, and Willow is carefully holding her dad's box as we walk to the stairs.

"Willow? Willow!" Dylan's voice is loud, and definitely not friendly.

"She has nothing to say to you," I reply, walking down the stairs in front of her.

"Who the fuck are you, and what are you doing in my house?" Dylan is standing at the foot of the stairs, hands on his hips.

"I'm getting *my* things from...our house." Willow's voice is clear and calm, even though I can tell she's terrified.

"You know it's too soon for you to check yourself out of rehab, sweetheart."

Obviously, he's sticking to his story for the sake of the staff, a handful of whom have gathered in various areas of the house, watching us.

"I was never in rehab, and you know it," she snaps.

"You can't just take things out of my house."

"*Our* house," she hisses, her step faltering.

I take her hand, draw her beside me then put a reassuring hand at her back.

"Keep walking," I encourage quietly.

"Tell me your name," Dylan turns his attention to me. "Because I'm going to have you brought up on kidnapping charges."

I chuckle. "Good luck with that. The name is Hudson Dash—do you need me to spell it for you?"

Chuck pulls a card out of his pocket and hands it to Dylan. "You can reach our office at any of those numbers. If you like, I can connect you with our attorney. Ms. St. Claire is a client so no laws are being broken here. Your housekeeper saw that Ms. St. Claire took only a handful of clothes and her father's keepsake box. Nothing of yours was taken."

Dylan turns back to me, narrowing his eyes. "Wait a minute—Hudson Dash. You operate Gamebreaker Security. Your services aren't cheap...you know she can't pay you, right?" The smirk on his face makes me want to knock him into the middle of next week.

That would be illegal, though.

And we have to do everything by the book if we're going to fight the conservatorship.

"Our compensation agreement is none of your business," I reply, gently pushing Willow behind me as we get to the bottom of the stairs.

"Her pussy isn't that magical," Dylan says dryly. "Frankly, it's about the most frigid cunt I've ever had the displeasure of fucking."

Fury boils inside me, but I cannot, under any circumstances, pummel him into the nearest wall. Or grind my fist into his stupid face. Or let Chuck and Ty give him the beatdown he deserves. No, we have to fight him in court. Which is going to be a lot more difficult.

"Let's go," I say to Willow, nodding at Ty, who moves toward the front door.

"My security guards can detain you." Dylan looks directly at Willow. "And in an hour you'll be back at the facility where you belong. Hiring a bodyguard isn't going to fix your issues—you know you need help, Willow. Resisting only means it's going to take longer to get you back to where you were before—where you belong. Where *I* can take care of you."

Willow shivers slightly, averting her gaze.

Dammit.

This is how he wears her down psychologically. Another few minutes and he'll potentially undo everything I've spent the last six weeks building up with her, and I'm not going to allow it.

"We're leaving," I say, nudging her forward.

Ty opens the front door, and as promised, there are three men standing by my black SUV.

Actually, it's kind of amusing because I can spot amateurs a mile away, and these guys are basically rent-a-cops. Ty could take out all three of them with one arm tied behind his back. Hell, so can I, even with the bum hip.

"Get in the back, babe." I speak softly, but I don't care who hears me.

Dylan Durand has no idea who he's messing with.

TWENTY

Willow

THE DRIVE back to Hudson's house is silent.

Tense. And silent.

"Thank you," I murmur to Ty and Chuck, Hudson's men who came with us to provide backup, as they carry in the suitcase and box of my father's things.

"Breathe easy, Willow," Ty murmurs, his big dark eyes gentle as they lock onto mine. "We've got your back."

I want to ask why.

Why these gentle giants of men—Ty and Chuck, Atlas and Hudson, Royal and Banks—have my back when for so many years the men in this industry have chewed me up and spit me out.

But I don't.

Because Hudson doesn't come close when he strides into the house several moments later, doesn't gently sweep my hair off my shoulder like he has been doing the last week or so, doesn't find some excuse to lightly touch my hand or back, doesn't even smile at me.

Instead, he walks right by me and disappears into the kitchen.

I jump when a cabinet slams.

I just force a smile at them, snag the handle of my suitcase, tuck my dad's box under my arm, and turn for the stairs.

"I can carry that up to your room for you," Chuck says softly, his hand landing on top of mine, staying me when I would have lifted the suitcase.

I slip my hand free, still not completely comfortable with men who aren't Hudson touching me. "I'm good," I murmur. "But thank you."

He studies me for a moment before he nods. "We'll arm the alarm before we go."

"Thank you," I say again.

He turns to Ty. "Let's go."

Ty's eyes flick to the kitchen, where Hudson disappeared, where there are more cabinets being opened and closed. Firmly. Still bordering on slamming. Still rubbing the wrong way against my nerves, making me jumpy and nervous. When they come back to mine there's worry edging into the brown depths, but he just reaches into his pocket then passes me a card that looks identical to the one he gave Dylan. "If you need anything else, feel free to call the office. Chuck and I are never far."

I nod, murmur another "thanks," and then I'm watching them slip out the front door, pausing to arm the alarm as promised. The lock *whirs* closed as Ty pushes a button on the keypad on the other side of the door.

Then I'm watching them walk away, disappear out of sight, and...

Silence falls.

But Hudson doesn't come back out into the entryway.

Exhaling softly, I wrap my fingers around the handle of my suitcase, decide to give him space, and make my way slowly upstairs.

I'm not one hundred percent in fighting shape quite yet—cardio is the devil—so my pulse is speeding by the time I make it up the stairs and carry my stuff down the hall and into the guest bedroom. Despite the newfound intimacy Hudson and I have had over the last week, I still have my stuff in the same room I've been occupying since I first began staying at Hudson's.

I don't know why it matters to me—to keep that distance—since we've been sleeping together in Hudson's bed every night since that first time together, since we spend pretty much every minute of our waking hours practically glued together.

It just...feels like too big of a step to keep anything in his room.

Too new. Too presumptuous. Too much too soon.

So, I've been coming back here to get dressed.

And it's where I unpack my suitcase, carefully organizing my clothes into the dresser drawers, but when I go to tuck the box of my dad's belongings carefully into the closet, I sense movement behind me.

Hudson is standing in the open doorway, eyes on my—now empty—suitcase.

They flick over to me as I set the box on the shelf and stand up.

"What the hell is this?" he mutters.

My eyebrows drag together. "What do you mean?"

"I mean," he snaps, moving toward me, "what are you doing putting your shit in the guest bedroom?"

I blink.

Then again.

"This is my room," I begin.

"Is it?" he growls.

"I—"

"Because it sure as shit hasn't been since the moment you climbed on top of me, princess."

More blinking.

"I was trying not to overstep."

"I've been inside you. I've kissed every inch of you." He's close now, near enough for me to see the flash of anger in his eyes. "I think we're well beyond overstepping, don't you?"

"I—" But I can't bring myself to agree with that, can't think too closely about that, or else I'll panic. Getting in this deep after Dylan? Insanity. And yet...it's Hudson, so I'm not exactly fighting the pull.

All of that is a whirlwind.

One I can't allow to take over.

So, I change the subject.

"You were mad on the drive home and downstairs."

"Yes," he agrees.

When he doesn't say anything else, I add, "You're mad about Dylan."

His eyes flash again and he steps closer. "Of course I'm mad about that asshole. He's an arrogant prick who hurt you, who tried to control you, right in fucking front of me, and who had your staff looking at you as though you're a criminal."

"I have a record." Or a juvenile one, anyway.

Hudson's expression turns to granite. "That doesn't give them—or him—the right to treat you like shit." He moves closer, extends an arm—

And I don't know if it was because I just saw Dylan or because I don't completely understand his mood. I don't know if it's the anger or the fierce lines hewn into his face. I don't know if it's just old habits brought to the surface.

But when he reaches toward me...

I flinch.

He freezes. *I* freeze, my insides tightening with horror.

"Christ, baby," he growls, his eyes flashing again, but this time with bone-deep hurt, "don't you know who I am by now?"

"I—"

"Fuck it." Shoving a hand through his hair, he spins on his heel, calls over his shoulder, "Do what you want. I have work to do."

I open my mouth again, trying to explain, trying to *apologize*.

But I don't get the chance.

He's already gone.

HUDSON DOESN'T COME HOME, and when the sun has set and my worry has ratcheted itself up to a hundred, I finally pull out my cell and hit the button to call Briar.

If anyone should understand Hudson, it's his sister.

She picks up on the second ring, the background so loud I actually hold my phone away from my ear. "Willow, hi. Just give me a second to move somewhere quiet."

"I can call back if this is a bad time."

"No," she says, the sounds slowly fading. "Royal, Jade, and Frankie are having a jam session, and while I love my baby girl and Royal and Jade—" I hear *whoosh* and then a click and the noise completely disappears. "I would sell my soul if I could have one evening of quiet."

Despite the worry knotting my insides, I find myself smiling. "I'm happy to babysit," I say. "Give you that quiet."

A blip of silence.

But before I can withdraw the offer—of course she doesn't

want a former mess of a child star with a dangerous ex to watch precious Frankie—she speaks.

"You're so incredibly nice, Willow. With all the shit you went through, how did that happen?"

My throat is tight. "I—"

"And be careful what you offer," she says lightly. "Because I'm one more rendition of 'Old MacDonald' away from leaving the country."

"Is Royal teaching her anything else?"

"Yes, thank God." She sighs. "Now we just need to convince her to play them—luckily Jade is on the case, and considering how much Frankie loves her, I hope my daughter will have a new repertoire before they leave tonight."

I giggle.

"Now, I'm sorry I hijacked the conversation. Did you need something or were you just calling to chat?"

"I..." My throat gets tight again, but she's patient, giving me a long time to get my words together.

When I don't manage to, her question is gentle, "Is this about the crap in the news? Atlas and Madeline are pissed, and them being pissed means that things are going to get done. This is all going to be over soon."

That's nice.

Really nice she's saying that. Really nice she's taking the time to reassure me.

And it unsticks me.

"I messed up."

"It's not your fault your ex—"

"With Hudson."

There's a moment of surprised silence then Briar gently asks, "How?"

I explain how we went back to my house, the confrontation

with Dylan, Hudson's sour mood. "And then he reached for me and I flinched."

"Oh, honey," she whispers.

"I hurt him," I whisper back. "I didn't mean to. I just... everything was fresh and I haven't seen him mad like that. And it's my fault."

"Honey," she says again, still gentle. "None of this is your fault. Dash is..." She sighs. "Did he talk to you about Colt?"

I nod, though she can't see me. "Yes," I say. "I'm sorry you guys lost him. He sounded like a really great guy."

There's another moment of silence and this time it's tinged with sadness.

"Yes," she finally says. "It was a hard loss for all of us." She exhales and seems to snap out of that melancholy. "But it was hardest for Dash. He and Colt were tighter than the rest, part of it was because they were deployed together, but part of it is because they just...gelled, you know?"

"Yeah," I murmur.

"So, when Colt enlisted for a final tour without talking to Dash—even though they'd agreed they were done—Dash was hurt. But when Colt didn't come back..." Her voice breaks. "I thought we'd lose him too. He was *undone.* He wasn't there to watch Colt's back. If he had been...then things would have been different. What he thinks," she adds. "Not any of us. Colt was stubborn and proud and what happened was a terrible tragedy. But none of that was my brother's fault."

My eyes burn.

Because he shared.

But not that.

"No," I agree, "it wasn't."

"Unfortunately, my brother isn't exactly known for being flexible."

My mouth curves up at that.

But she's still talking and the next words take my breath away. "The man I saw at Sunday Dinner wasn't the Dash of the last four years," she says softly, and my pulse begins to pick up its pace. "He's been lost, honey. Lost and alone and sometimes so impenetrable I feared I'd never get my brother back."

That makes my heart hurt, so freaking much. "I'm sorry."

"Me too," Briar whispers. "But you need to know that *you* brought him back, sweetheart. He was our Dash again, and that's because of you. The way he looked at you, the jokes he made, the laughter and care and lightness in him—even though all that you're both dealing with is so heavy—that's not the closed-off man who's been here the last few years. God, that mess you two made in the kitchen alone was enough proof of that—"

"He started it," I blurt.

She laughs, which was my intention. Because her voice was watery and it was making my throat go tight again and...

I don't want her to be sad.

"I bet he did," she says, still laughing. "And I'm so damned glad he was himself enough to do it."

I suck in a breath.

"So, you didn't mess up, honey. He's a protector, through and through, and hates what you endured. But he's not mad at you—not really."

He's mad at Dylan.

And that I was hurt.

"I know," I say and I mean it. "I just...he's been so great. I hate that I hurt him, even a little bit."

"Because you're a good person."

Stated so matter-of-factly that it penetrates deep, settles right around my heart.

I've always heard how bad I am, how incapable, how pathetic. But not good. *Never* good.

And yet, this wonderful woman states it so easily.

Maybe that's why I can believe it.

But even as I'm accepting that, I know it's not just Briar's statement. It's Hudson. His faith, his patience, his kindness, all working together to make it so I can hold those words close, can tuck them inside me and keep them safe.

"You are too," I murmur.

We're both quiet for a couple of seconds but then I hear Frankie's voice in the background.

"Your moment of quiet is over?" I ask lightly.

A beleaguered sigh—but it's filled with amusement. "Apparently."

"Before you go," I say. "I did have just one more question..."

TWENTY-ONE

Dash

SOMETHING DELICIOUS HITS my nostrils the minute I come through the door, and my feet propel me toward the kitchen. I don't know what's cooking but I hope it's done because it's been a long day and I'm tired, starving, and a little frustrated.

I was mad earlier but now that I've had time to think, I understand why she flinched. Why she needs more time—and probably a fuck ton of therapy—to move past the emotional and physical abuse Dylan put her through. Years of abuse isn't going to disappear overnight, and I have to remember that.

And give us both a little grace.

"Hi." She whirls as I walk into the kitchen, but there's no fear in her eyes now.

Now all I see is...regret?

I hate that too.

"Hey. I just wanted—" I begin.

"I need to—" She starts talking at the same time.

We both smile.

"Ladies first," I say politely.

"I need to apologize. I'm so sorry I reacted the way I did. It wasn't about you so much as what Dylan said and—"

"It was absolutely about him." I cut her off and slowly hold out my hand, waiting for her to take it. "I understand that now, princess."

Instead of taking my hand, she throws herself against my chest.

"I'm sorry, Hudson. Truly sorry. I didn't mean to hurt your feelings."

My arms close around her, and I inhale the scent of her hair, pressing soft kisses on her temple. She feels so damn good. "Shh. You don't have to apologize. I'm the one who's sorry. I was mad at him, but I took it out on you. That was wrong."

"It's okay. I guess we both freaked out a little." She rests her head against my chest, and everything falls into place. This is how it's supposed to be.

We're quiet for a minute or so before she whispers, "I missed you all day."

"I missed you too."

And I did.

Normally, when I'm at work, I don't think about anyone or anything else—but today, Willow was basically all I thought about.

Suddenly she whirls. "Shit! The garlic bread." She grabs a pot holder and throws open the oven, pulling out a tray of cheese-covered bread. It's a little brown but still makes my mouth water.

"That looks awesome," I say, leaning over with interest.

"Briar told me veal parmesan was your favorite." She lifts a platter out of the lower oven, since the garlic bread was in the upper.

"God, that looks amazing. Let me wash my hands and we can eat."

"Perfect. I set the table in the dining room...I thought we'd be a little fancy tonight."

"Sounds great." I move to the sink and have just put my hands under the water when I hear her gasp.

"Where's your boot?!"

I chuckle. "That's one of the reasons I had to leave in such a hurry—I was late for my appointment to find out if I can stop wearing it and didn't want to miss it. I'll need some PT for the ankle, but Doc says I'm good to go."

"That's wonderful." She smiles, and it lights up the fucking room.

I am so gone for this woman.

Watching her in my kitchen putting the garlic bread in a bread basket, wearing jeans and a T-shirt with bare feet, just pounds home the fact that she's where she belongs—with me.

Dinner is amazing, and I can't help but shake my head.

"I thought you didn't know how to cook."

Pink cheeks. "Briar dished on the recipe...and some YouTube videos I could follow step-by-step."

I grin. For a rich, spoiled Hollywood starlet, she's full of surprises. Of course, I now know her public persona is nothing like the woman she really is. That other person is who Dylan Durand wants everyone to *think* she is, but I know better.

I know more about her after six weeks than the rest of the world knows despite watching her since she was a child. It's a little heady to have this kind of intimacy with one of the most famous women in Hollywood, but it also feels comfortable. Like we've been together a lot longer than we have.

I've never experienced this with another woman.

Never imagined it could feel like this to be with someone special.

"I did some redecorating while you were gone," she says as we eat.

"Oh?" I arch a brow. I don't care if she painted the whole house purple, as long as she's happy.

"I moved out of the guest room." Her eyes meet mine, and the fire there is both satisfying and sexy.

"Yeah?" I feign nonchalance. "Where'd you move to?"

She makes a playful face. "Your room, silly."

I frown like I'm confused. "Which room is that?"

She momentarily falters. "Wh-what do you mean?"

I shrug. "I don't have a room. *We* have a room, though."

Her face softens and tears glisten in her eyes. "Hudson..." She puts down her fork and blinks a few times. But I don't want her to be upset.

"Don't cry, princess." I reach out and run my knuckles across her cheek. "I want you here. You know that, don't you? This isn't about being your bodyguard. I have half a dozen safe houses and corporate apartments all over the state where I could put you, where you would be safe. There's only one reason I'd keep you here—with me."

She swallows, eyes never leaving mine. "Are we... is this..." She stops talking and closes her eyes, as if rethinking what she wants to say. "I mean, I feel it too. I just don't want to assume... Dylan is the only man I've ever been in a relationship with as an adult. And I don't want you to feel trapped because you feel—"

"Trapped?" I stare at her. "Are you serious, princess? You think I'd let myself be trapped if I didn't want to be? I'm crazy about you. From the minute I saw you lying there in that hospital bed, something pulled at me. And that was before I knew you were Willow St. Claire. The woman lying there spoke to my soul. Believe me, I know how ridiculous that sounds but—"

"It's *not* ridiculous. From the moment you started to read to me, I knew you were special. I didn't know you, but your voice broke through the coma, the subconscious part of me that was too afraid to come out of the darkness because I knew what was waiting for me. But then there was you. You were waiting in the light and that gave me the strength to come back." Her eyes glisten with tears again. "My soul was listening, Hudson."

I lean over and brush my lips across hers.

We stare at each other for a beat, and then dinner is forgotten. I get to my feet and then lift her right out of her chair. Her legs close around me as our mouths fuse together.

Fuck, I want her all the damn time.

I push her against the nearest wall, kissing her like I'm about to stake a claim. Her lips are sweet, the faint taste of wine from dinner lingering, and our tongues swirl with familiarity and heat. She's so passionate when she lets herself go, and watching her come undone has become my favorite pastime.

"Bedroom," I grunt, letting her slide to the ground. I'm not supposed to carry more than fifty pounds yet—and while she's slender, I don't want to risk it.

She doesn't seem to be worried about whether or not I carry her, because she grabs my hand and we practically fly up the stairs.

We're ripping each other's clothes off the minute we get to my—*our*—room, and she grabs a condom before throwing herself on the bed. We're a tangle of limbs and lips and groping hands, touching and kissing and climbing all over each other. She's finding herself again, and I love being the man who brings out her passionate side.

She has one long leg wrapped around my middle and I grind my cock against her core, making her moan.

"Hudson, I need you..."

I just kiss her some more in response, plunging my tongue

deep into her mouth as she wiggles and writhes against me. I slip two fingers between her legs and she's drenched—for me. This never gets old, knowing—feeling—how much she wants me. She may look fragile and delicate, but when we're together like this, she burns with sensuality and passion.

So maybe it's time to up the intensity.

I like it a little rough, but I've held back with Willow, wanting to earn her trust and learn what she likes. But it feels like she needs more from me and I want to give her anything and everything she needs.

I grab her hands, lifting them over her head, and holding them firmly in one of mine as I roll us over so I'm on top.

She wiggles and twists her head. "Hudson, don't—"

"My hip is fine, princess," I growl. "Now let me—"

"Hudson, no!" Her cry of distress pierces my lusty haze and I freeze.

"Princess?"

"Stop, no! Let me go!" Her eyes are wide and no longer filled with the desire of a few seconds ago.

I immediately let go of her hands. "Willow, what's—"

"Get off me!" She pushes at my chest and I roll to the side, trying to figure out what's going on.

"Honey, can you please—"

She's not listening.

In fact, she's in full-on panic mode.

The moment she's free of me she practically leaps off the bed and runs to the bathroom, slamming the door shut behind her.

Leaving me staring in confusion.

What the hell just happened?

TWENTY-TWO

Willow

MY HEAD IS A MESS—MEMORIES swirling, their barbed edges slicing at me, panic gripping so tightly that my vision goes splotchy and I find that my legs can't hold me up.

I sink to the floor, but don't have the strength to slow my descent, my knees cracking hard against the tile.

Hard enough that Hudson's concerned voice cuts through the closed door.

"Princess!"

The handle rattles, but apparently in my panic I locked it behind me.

And I don't have the strength to get up and unlock it.

Nor do I want to.

Because the memories are swirling and panic is stealing my breath, making me light-headed and my vision narrow to tiny points of light.

Because...shame is washing over me.

I messed up. *Again.*

Only this wasn't a flinch.

This was me ruining a beautiful moment between us.

My eyes burn, and I wrap an arm around my aching knees, settling my forehead on top of them.

Why am I like this?

Why do I always ruin everything?

"Willow," Hudson says through the closed door. "Baby, please talk to me."

And say what? That I'm weak and pathetic and stupid and—

No!

I don't even know where that thought comes from.

But it's sharp enough to snap me out of my panic, out of the self-loathing.

I'm not that woman anymore.

I'm not weak. I'm not pathetic. I'm not stupid.

"Willow!"

I'm too busy having a breakthrough.

Instead of a damned break*down*.

Apparently, though, Hudson is out of patience.

With a *thunk* and a *crack*, the door pops open, and I look up in time to see a big hand catching it before it can slam into the opposite wall.

He moves slower then, carefully stepping into the opening.

His hazel eyes are unreadable as he takes in the sight of me on the floor, but he doesn't say anything, and when he slips out of the opening, disappearing from view, my heart leaps, terror slicing my insides to ribbons.

But he's not gone for long.

Almost as soon as that worry builds, it wanes again.

Because he's back, pants on, something clenched in his hand as he slowly moves into the bathroom, crouching near me.

His T-shirt, I realize a heartbeat later as he passes it over to me.

"Put it on, princess," he murmurs. "You're shivering."

I am, I realize, taking the material and tugging it over my head. It helps a little, but I'm not cold, not exactly.

It's cool in here and the tile isn't comfortable and warm beneath me.

But the shivering is because of the adrenaline.

"Here, baby," he says, still soft, still quiet, and I look up to see him holding up a blanket.

My heart spasms, eyes burning again, and I can't move.

Thankfully, he does it for me, slowly—oh so slowly—wrapping the blanket around me.

The warmth settles over me and eventually the shaking begins to calm. But after we've sat in silence for long minutes, the voices begin rising again, reminding me what I did, how I acted, why we're sitting here—

"Can I hold you?" he whispers.

My throat is tight, so I just nod, those sharp edges inside of me filed down when he draws me close.

"I'm sorry." I drop my head to his shoulder. "I ruined it."

He's quiet for several heartbeats then his big chest inflates and deflates. "I was kind of coming in here to apologize for doing just that."

I shake my head. "It wasn't your fault. I..." I take a deep breath. "I was the one who freaked out."

He cups my jaw, turns my face up so our gazes meet. "I pushed too far, too fast, princess. That's on me." A flicker of steel in his eyes. "And I won't make that same mistake again."

My heart skips a beat as I remember my conversation with Briar earlier.

His thumb smooths lightly over my cheek. "In the kitchen I

was thinking about how strong you are and how much you've been through and how far you've come in such little time."

Another pulse through my middle.

I want to look away, want to tell him he's wrong, that the evidence of my weakness is written right here in the fact that we're sitting on the bathroom floor after an aborted love making session.

But his hand is on my jaw and I find I can't tear my eyes from his.

"You're strong, baby, and you've been through hell. We need to remember that it's not just going to be easy moving forward."

I sigh.

His voice lightens, humor creeping into his eyes. "And I need to remember myself when you're being so fucking sexy that I stop thinking."

My stomach clenches again. "But I want you to be able to stop thinking. I want you to be able to forget yourself and do the things in bed"—my cheeks heat—"that you want without me limiting—"

"Stop, baby," he orders roughly. "You're not limiting me."

I nod.

"You're *not*."

I nod again. "Except for the fact that I freaked out and ran into the bathroom."

"So we need to take things slow," he says, dropping his hand from my jaw. "There's fun in taking things slow."

"Except if you want to take them fast and your partner can't keep up." And I don't honestly know if I *can* keep up with all that Hudson wants and needs in a relationship. I flinch at his touch, freak out in bed.

I'm messed up.

I'm traumatized.

I—

I stare into his hazel eyes but I can't read the emotions in the unfathomable depths.

And then he slowly lets me go and stands up, moves away from me.

Damn.

A pang through my middle, my heart convulsing, my eyes burning. My lids slide closed and I drop my chin to my chest.

"Princess."

They fly open, see that Hudson is there—right there—and his hand is extended toward me.

"Will you come with me?"

I can't deny him that.

I can't deny him anything—not when he's looking at me with those soft eyes, talking to me with that gentle voice.

I nod, allow him to draw me to my feet.

He slips the blanket from my shoulders, but passes me a pair of my pajama pants, tugs a sweatshirt over my head.

It's so big, it practically engulfs me, but being wrapped in his scent settles me enough that I don't protest when he tugs on a pair of socks, my shoes, and draws me downstairs to the garage.

Minutes later, we're driving through the dark, the quiet roads all but deserted.

It's not until he's pulling to a stop on a moonlit overlook that I understand.

Heart pounding, I turn to him.

"You came here after Colt died."

TWENTY-THREE

Dash

SHE ALREADY KNOWS ME. Gets me.

It's a little uncanny how intuitive she is—how thoughtful.

Even in the midst of her own trauma, she's cognizant of mine.

And I fall a little harder. A little deeper.

I'm already tied up in knots over this woman, ready to do anything and everything to keep her. This instinctive empathy is going to do me in.

"Yeah," I say after a moment. "This was my spot. For the first few months after Colt died this was the only place I could breathe. He loved the water so when I was here I felt like he was with me."

"That must have been so painful," she whispers, leaning closer to me.

"I can't even..." Damn, even now, four years later, it's hard to talk about him. Think about him. Remember him. "I still hear his voice sometimes. His laugh. The way he'd grunt when we used to wrestle and fight... It's been four years but I still reach for the phone sometimes."

"I can't imagine your loss."

"And the guilt. I know it's not my fault. He made a unilateral decision. The Special Forces thing is hardcore, and you have to break all ties for a while if you want to be able to focus. But out of all of us, I'm the one who understands all that. I lived part of it with him, so not telling me what he was going to do hurt."

"He knew you were meant for something else," she says gently. "And he was afraid you would follow him into whatever hell he was going to."

"He was right, I guess. If I'd known, I would have gone too. I could have—should have—been with him, had his back."

"Maybe, but there's every possibility that it wouldn't have been enough and now you would both be dead. And Frankie would be down two uncles instead of just one."

I never thought of it quite that way.

"Yeah... I mean, Banks, Atlas, and Royal would have made sure she and Briar lacked for nothing, but I would hate not being in her life."

"So maybe Colt did you a favor, in his own way."

"I just wish I'd had a chance to say goodbye. We didn't leave things on good terms. He just...left. Without a word. I didn't know he'd gone until after. He had some money, assets... asked me to take care of things in case something went bad."

"Did he leave everything to you?"

I frown for a second. "He left everything to Briar and me, split equally. Since he didn't have any family, and the other guys didn't need it, his letter said it would help Briar get her start in life and would help me in whatever I planned to do after the military."

"Did it?"

"Help me start my security firm? Yeah. And when Frankie's dad left them high and dry, it came in handy for them too. Again, the four of us were never going to let them want for anything, but I think she liked having something that was hers. That she didn't have to ask us for. Then Atlas hired her and she took that bull by the horns."

A faint smile touches Willow's lips. "So Colt left part of him with you. And if you still think about him, hear his voice in your head, then he's always with you."

"It's getting harder," I admit. "I think about him, and I can still hear his voice sometimes, but other times... I start to forget. Now that we're all busy and successful, taking care of Frankie, doing our own things—I don't think about him as often. And I'm scared that..." I break off, unwilling to say the words aloud.

"Scared that you'll forget him?" She squeezes my hand. "Never. You know that. He's part of you."

"I have videos—from college and when we were in the military together—so I play them sometimes... to make sure I keep his memory alive."

"I'd love to see one sometime. So I can meet him too." Her voice is soft, filled with genuine interest.

"Would you?" I stare at her as she nods.

I get out my phone and open the app where everything is saved.

There are lots of videos. Not as many as I would have liked, but we were always doing dumb shit in college. I want her to "meet" the real Colt, though. Not drunk Colt, or obnoxious hockey player Colt.

Christmas.

Our last Christmas together.

We'd been in Afghanistan that year, unable to get home because we were supposed to be separating from the military in a few months.

"Here," I say, pressing the button. "We recorded this for Briar and the guys."

"Merry Christmas, guys!" My voice comes on first and Colt pops up from behind me, shirtless and wearing a Santa hat.

"Merry Christmas, you fuckers!" he yells. "Except Briar. Merry Christmas, sweetie."

"Sorry we couldn't get home for the holidays," I continue.

"But we'll be home in time for your graduation, Briar!" Colt is grinning, his eyes twinkling with amusement. "And I have a present for you."

"I hope you got the stuff we ordered," I say into the camera. "It wasn't much but we wanted you to know we were thinking about all of you."

"Hey, they get to see my cute face," Colt interjects, laughing. "What more do they need?"

I watch as I roll my eyes, shaking my head at him. "Put a shirt on, you loser."

"Why? My nips offend you?"

"Shut up."

Our banter was second nature—even when filming a holiday video for friends and family.

"By the way—the cookies were awesome, Briar," Colt says, nodding. "I had to hide a few before fatso here ate them all."

"Fuck all the way off!" I say, elbowing him.

"Ow!" Colt yelps, grabs his side, and pretends to collapse in pain.

"Asshole...sorry, gang. Anyway, we just wanted to send this so you'd have it when you wake up, because we have to go on patrol soon."

"Hey, for real, we'll be home in April," Colt says, popping back up, "and I'm looking forward to some ice time together, boys. I'm about done with this desert heat. Oh, and maybe more cookies—because they're really the bomb, Briar. Thank you." And for a few seconds, he's being completely serious and sincere, something we didn't see from him very often.

"We miss you," I say. "And we'll be home soon. Merry Christmas."

"Merry Christmas, everyone. Miss you."

The video ends and I feel a weird scratching behind my eyes.

Fuck.

This is why I don't watch the videos very often—it hits me right in the gut every time.

"He was handsome," Willow says softly. "And funny."

"Yeah, he was a hoot. And the ladies seemed to agree with your assessment."

"Thank you for playing that for me." When I look up there are tears in her eyes too, but she's smiling. "I think I would have liked him."

"He would have liked you too." I smile fondly. "He would be giving me so much shit right now... you're sleeping with Willow St. Claire? What the fuck, dude? She's way too hot for you..."

She giggles. "Well, if he were here, I would set him straight about that. I happen to think you're incredibly hot, Mr. Dash."

I lean over and brush my lips across hers. "Thank you for sharing that with me."

"Always." She grins, then her expression goes serious and she puts her hand on the side of my face. "I like that I can be here for you the way you've been there for me. And I'm really sorry about... earlier."

"You don't have anything to be sorry about. I should have asked you if bondage is something you're comfortable with. I figured since it was me, just my hands holding yours, it wasn't like you were actually restrained. But I should have asked. And I apologize for that."

"He used to..." She huffs out a breath.

"What?" I ask gently. "You can tell me anything."

"I know. It's just...hard to think about."

"Tell me what he did so I can make sure I never even come close to doing the same things."

"It would never be the same with you," she whispers, lowering her gaze.

I don't say anything, giving her time to gather her thoughts. My chest is tight again, like it is every time she talks about him, because I can't imagine having this sweet, gorgeous, giving woman in your life and your bed, and mistreating her. For no apparent reason.

"He used to tie me up," she blurts, her fingers suddenly icy cold in mine. "He would... have sex with me and then... leave me there. Sometimes until the next day... until Mrs. Wilkes..." She cuts off and horror fills me.

The urge to hurt someone—not Willow, *never* Willow—is so strong I have to start mentally counting to ten.

What in the ever-loving fuck is wrong with that guy?

Someday, some place—I'm going to make him pay for every single time he hurt her.

"I would never do that," I say, my voice thick with emotions I'm struggling to understand. Not just the fury at the way he treated her but also my own need to make sure no one hurts her ever again.

A thought tickles my psyche—a story she told me about Dylan forcing her to work out even when she had walking pneumonia—and the possessiveness that washes over me is impossible to deny.

I'll do anything it takes to protect her from him.

"I know." She still won't look at me. "I just remembered... the first time... Mrs. Wilkes came in and I was naked... on the bed. Spread eagle. And she acted like it was no big deal. Like this is something he does all the time. The only reason she went and got Dylan to let me go is because I told her I was going to pee all over the bed."

"Mother—" I try to hide my anger, so she doesn't think it's directed at her, but it's infuriating.

"I'm sure that was his plan... to get me pregnant. To just keep me in bed until it was too late."

"He's never going to touch you again," I vow. "You have my word on that, Willow. I will end him before he can ever lay another hand on you."

I'm a thousand percent serious too.

TWENTY-FOUR

Willow

I HAVE two palms full of bread dough a couple of days later when my phone rings.

"Dammit," I whisper.

I have dough to knead and food to finish prepping, a nice meal to put together for Hudson and Frankie, since we're on babysitting duty for a few hours tonight. And I want to have it all ready before he gets back with his niece in tow.

We're having fancy food—at Frankie's request.

So, I've upped my YouTube recipe watching, spent lots of time practicing, and tonight we're having homemade bread (loaded with garlic and cheddar cheese), marinated chicken breasts (they're currently soaking in a delicious brine in the fridge), veggies that are cut prettily and spices (though not too much because she's four and I don't want to overwhelm her tastebuds), and scalloped potatoes (the slender slices carefully arranged in a pan, topped with cream and cheese and ready to be baked next to me).

Is it overkill for a meal, even a fancy one that a preschooler requested? Yes. But am I slowly going insane not having anything to do around Hudson's house?

I've tried cleaning and organizing—but he has a housekeeper, so that didn't take long.

Even the baseboards were free of dust.

And he's not the kind of man to hoard junk that needs to be tossed or donated.

I've read until my eyes hurt, swam laps in his pool, used the gym on the ground floor. And while I might be stronger than I've been in years—even stronger than when I played a gunslinging cowgirl a few films back—I'm slowly going insane.

Hudson has work, and while I know he would do it here—would *be* here—if I asked, he has a life and a business and clients to look after.

And I have...

Well, my safety. Time to get my head together, to let Hudson and Atlas and Madeline and Kate work their magic on my behalf, and while I'm beyond grateful, while I know how lucky I am to have it...

I'm slowly going insane.

I don't have a script to memorize. I don't have reshoots. I don't have meetings to discuss future projects.

I've worked since I was a child.

Yes, I've taken breaks, but those breaks were always punctuated with what I would be doing next.

Even in my darkest days, there was always the next party, the next drama, the next high.

This peaceful existence—no matter how wonderfully safe—is beginning to make my skin itch.

I *need* to do something.

Today, that's make a fancy three-course meal for a four-year-old and my boyfriend.

(And the third course is positively decadent—a four-layer chocolate cake filled with hazelnut mousse, salted caramel, and covered with a whipped ganache frosting.)

Tomorrow...

Well, I'll figure it out.

Because if there's anything I've learned about myself, that I've learned to trust over these last weeks, it's that I *will* figure it out.

Maybe not alone.

But that's okay too.

My phone rings again and I set the dough onto the floured board, reach over and swipe a dirty finger across the screen.

Unfortunately, I do this without looking at the caller ID because I'm focused on the bread. It needs its final rise before cooking can fully commence and the call has interrupted the transfer of my carefully formed loaf to the pan where it can complete that rise.

"Hello?" I say as I scoop the dough back up and gingerly settle it in the pan.

There's silence.

Long enough for my annoyance to grow and my scowl to deepen. If I've lost the air bubbles I've laboriously...well, *labored* to keep and my bread is heavy, there will be hell to pay.

"Hello?" I repeat as I cover the loaf with a towel, reach for my phone to disconnect what is obviously a spam call—

But my finger doesn't make it.

Because I freeze when the voice comes through the phone.

"What the fuck do you think you're doing?"

Thank God, the dough is safe.

Thank God, I don't have a knife in my hand.

Thank God, I'm not the woman I was mere weeks before.

"Mother," I say coldly, dumping the floured board into the sink and reaching for the vegetables I've already prewashed.

Fuck it, I'm employing my knife skills.

"I repeat," she snaps. "What the fuck are you doing?"

"Why don't you start by telling me what it is you think I'm doing?"

"Dylan says—"

"I'm not using again," I growl, lining up green beans and efficiently trimming their ends.

Thank God, I played a chef once on a short-lived TV series.

Even with my blood pressure soaring and new rage filling me—my mother is calling me *now*? After everything?—I'm fairly confident that I'll keep all my fingers.

Even when she scoffs and says, "Once an addict, always an addict."

Same shit, different day.

I exhale, reach for my patience, but I don't manage to grasp it, my tone sharp when I ask, "How'd you get this number?"

"You know there's any number of ways to open up all sorts of doors."

In other words, she bribed someone to get it—or Dylan did.

Ugh.

"What do you need, Mom?" I say on a sigh, making a mental note to pass this information along to Hudson. "More money?"

There's a long moment of tense silence. "You have a lot of nerve, girl."

"*I* have a lot of nerve?" I ask, and it's like now that I've begun, I can't stop. All of the little injustices are flashing through my mind, one after another like a fucked-up slideshow. "Have I misremembered and you're the one who paid for your house? And that last cruise you took? And the new car you got last year?"

My mom has her problems, but I've always supported her.

And I never was resentful of it.

Or was never *aware* of that resentment.

Because it's sure as fuck blaring to the forefront of my consciousness right here and now.

"That's beside the point," she says. "We need to talk about poor Dylan about what you're doing to him."

"Poor Dylan?" I grit out, my anger reaching volcanic proportions. "*Poor Dylan?*"

I set the knife down.

And look at that, I've rage-finished the green beans in record time.

"Yes, *poor Dylan,*" she snaps.

I reach for the peeler, dump the tiny organic carrots I've left the stems on onto the cutting board, and start sheering off their tough exteriors. "Tell me how the man who has financially and physically abused me over the last years deserves *any* amount of sympathy."

There's the barest moment of silence, as though I've taken her by surprise.

But just as quickly, she pulls the wool back over her own eyes and gets lost in her delusions. "Well, I'm sure that whatever measures Dylan needed to take were necessary."

"It was necessary to hit me?" I ask. "To sexually assault me? To"—I close my eyes, peeler pause—"to rape me? To punch me so hard that I ended up in a coma?"

Another pause. "You need to get clean, baby girl."

My eyes fly open and I know it's pointless to continue this conversation. She won't believe me—not today, not ever. And I don't know if it's because she's getting paid by my estate or she just believes that the sun shines out of Dylan's ass, but...

She's never going to believe me.

"Why did you do it?" I ask quietly.

There's a long blip of quiet.

"You need to go home," she goes on. "You need to go home to Dylan so he can help you with all of that."

"Why did you sign everything over to Dylan?" I press. "Why did you take away all of my power, tie up my money and assets? I did the work. I was taking care of you and myself—"

I got clean.

I'd lined up jobs.

"He was good for you. Stabilizing and he looked after you."

Maybe if she'd done it when I didn't need it so much, I would understand, would buy that.

But I'd been doing better.

And then she took away my freedom, just signed it right over to the devil.

"You know that's not true."

She scoffs. "He's the only reason you have the career you have today, the only reason you can live as though you do—"

And I get it then.

Because eventually the Bank of Willow would have closed.

My mother was protecting *herself*.

And just like that...

I'm done.

"I'm done," I repeat aloud.

"What—?"

"I'm done with this conversation, done with you, done with it all." I exhale. "Don't call me again. Not today. Not next year. Not ever."

"Willow—"

I reach out and hit the button to end the call.

And then reject the next one when she immediately calls back.

And *then* I block her, and maybe I should be sad but for the first time in a decade the persistent heaviness in my heart is gone. Because...

"I'm not her anymore," I whisper.

Not just a child star. Not just a victim of the industry. Not just a teenager with too much access and too few boundaries. Not just a woman who faced and survived unspeakable horrors.

I'm strong and capable and successful.

I'm kind and respectful and talented.

I'm Willow Fucking St. Claire.

That's enough.

I smile and hold that close.

And then I make some fancy fucking princess food for a little girl who's all of that and more.

TWENTY-FIVE

Dash

TODAY WAS my first day on an actual assignment. It was light work, taking a legendary octogenarian Hollywood actress to the doctor. She's been my client from the beginning, and at ninety-one years young is still pretty spry. She always flirts with me shamelessly and almost lost her mind when she found out I'd been injured. I had to give her every detail of my surgery and recovery, and somehow, I found myself telling her all about Willow.

Her brows lifted way up on her forehead. "Willow... St. Claire?" she asked in her British accent. "What a beautifully damaged young woman."

"She's not damaged," I muttered. "Unless you count the physical bruises that bastard left on her."

This time her brows knitted with concern. "*Dylan Durand*. Never liked him. Wanker."

I smiled. "I'm protecting her—and in the process falling for her."

This made her smile, forcing the entire story out of me even though it was only a fifteen-minute drive to the doctor's office.

"Take care of her," she whispered when I dropped her off. "And not just her body. Her mind, her soul, all of her. She may look like a princess living in a gilded cage, but she's a human being. And if she's not ill, then she needs the world to see it. Trust me on this, Hudson. The best response is for everyone to see her living her best life." She patted my arm, kissed my cheek, and smiled before closing the door.

And I've thought of nothing else.

Has it been a mistake keeping Willow cooped up in my very safe, very private house? Where no one can find her, see her, or do anything to hurt her? She's been antsy the last few days, and I feel bad, but I'm also afraid of what Dylan might do if he gets his hands on her. Afraid he'll take her where even *I* can't find her—and then what?

The smell of something amazing hits my nostrils the minute I walk in and I smile. She's gotten serious about learning to cook and the results have been incredible. I'm going to have to spend a lot more time on the treadmill if she keeps this up.

"Hey, babe." I walk into the kitchen and press my lips to hers.

"Hi." She kisses me back but quickly turns away, grabbing a potholder and pulling something out of the oven.

"What is it today?" I ask with interest.

"Osso Buco."

Braised veal shanks? Yes, please.

"Holy... you've upped the stakes to a point I may have to fire Judith and hire you instead." Judith is my housekeeper.

"Well, I'm going to need to start earning money again," she replies, laughing. "I can think of worse jobs."

"Do you... miss acting?" I ask carefully.

She nods. "Absolutely. But I don't know that Hollywood is going to welcome me back with open arms. Not with the slaughter job Dylan has done to my reputation."

"We're going to fix it," I say. "In fact, we're going to dinner with Atlas and Madeline tomorrow night to talk about it."

"We are?" She frowns. "Where?"

"Atlas made a reservation at Craig's for tomorrow evening."

Her eyes round. "*Craig's?* But we can't... I mean, I can't..." She sputters and then seems to catch herself. She lifts her chin a tiny bit. "Is that a good idea?"

"Why not? It's a trendy Los Angeles restaurant where affluent people go for good food and a nice atmosphere. Is that not us?"

She seems to be taking it in. Mulling it over. As if this is some kind of monumental decision. And I have to let her sort it out.

"Madeline says it's her favorite," I add in a cajoling voice.

She still doesn't react.

"Babe?" Now I'm getting a little worried.

"What am I going to wear?" she finally asks. "I didn't bring anything for...going out to dinner."

"Then I guess we should go shopping. In the morning."

She doesn't say anything but comes over and wraps her arm around my middle. And in the quietest voice whispers, "Thank you."

We pull up to Craig's in my SUV. Ty is driving and will be on duty tonight since I don't trust Dylan not to try something. I can handle myself, and so can Atlas, but I can't handle a situation discreetly while simultaneously making sure Willow and Madeline are also safe, so this is an easier solution.

For some reason, Willow seems taken with Ty—in a sweet, platonic way, I'm in no way jealous—and him with her. He came back from Afghanistan with a slew of ghosts and she battles her own, and they seem to have found a connection. God knows, she needs friends, so I'm happy to indulge her in this. Well, in anything, really.

If she's happy, I'm happy.

Once we're seated and wine has been poured, Atlas wastes no time in getting us up to speed.

"Unfortunately," he says with a scowl, "your bank account is currently empty."

"Empty?" She blinks. "What are you talking about? How can it be...empty?"

"That bottom feeder obviously transferred everything to his personal accounts."

Willow pulls in a shaky breath and it's obvious she's on the verge of tears, but before I can do something, she juts out her jaw. "How do we get it back?" she demands in a quiet but steely voice.

Atlas almost smiles—it happens rarely. Usually only for Frankie. Or if he fucks over someone who's tried to fuck him over. He's terrifying if you don't know him as well as I do.

"Well, let's get the bad news out of the way first," Madeline says, her tone easygoing but careful.

"There's more bad news beyond me being completely broke?" Willow sighs.

"Dylan has gotten a restraining order against you."

"Against *me*?" Willow gapes at her.

"Basically he's trying to make sure you can't get any more of your things by showing up at the house when he's not there. And I believe he's attending some film festival next week, so this is his way of making sure you can't take anything else."

Atlas makes a strangled sound—like he wants to hurt

someone—and I'm right there with him, but I try to mask my anger for Willow's sake.

"Fuck him," she mutters.

"Exactly." Madeline pulls some papers out of her bag. "So. We've officially retained Kate Martensson, the crisis control manager, and she's got a few things in the works. First, Alexa Humboldt is holding a ladies' only tea on Sunday, giving attendees first dibs at her new line. It's one hundred women, including some of her wealthiest and most trusted clients. Kate got you on the list."

"But you just told me I'm broke?" Willow looks at me and holds up a finger before I can talk. "Don't you dare say you'll pay for it!"

I hold up my hands in surrender. "No, dear. Absolutely not. I would never."

She makes a face. "Hudson..."

"You two can bicker later," Madeline says. "This is on my dime, as part of our campaign to fix your image and get you back out there. I'm certain Atlas and Hudson can cover it if you try to dodge the bill."

Willow flushes.

Money is such a difficult topic for her, and short-term, there's nothing I can do to fix that.

"That bastard robbed her," I growl. "I mean, how is this legal?"

"He has legal control. Her mother set it up when she was a minor, and she's never challenged it as an adult."

"Can I challenge it now?" Willow asks.

"Of course. That's what we're getting ready to do. But first, we start fixing your image. Sunday is the private tea, and I believe sometime next week you're all going to see some country star perform?"

Atlas rolls his eyes but nods. "Yes. Jade set it up. We'll be backstage and at an after party of some kind with Lily Maxwell. They're good friends."

"Oh!" Willow's face brightens. "I love her music. She's wonderful. How exciting that I'll get to meet her."

"And you're also going to throw Aspen a baby shower," I say. "I mean, Briar is throwing it, but we're switching it up to say you and Briar are throwing it together."

Madeline is making notes. "Yes, Kate is going to attend and make sure lots of curated photos flood social media."

"Is...Aspen okay with that?" Willow asks.

"She is if it helps you," Atlas responds.

"And it appears that I'm going to have a cold at the next Vipers game," I say, shrugging. "Briar and Atlas will be out of town, so you, Jade, and Aspen are taking Frankie."

"Lots of ladies-only events," Willow muses. "This is by design?"

"It's easy to show that a beautiful woman can get a man," Madeline says pragmatically. "But making girlfriends is harder. And children up the ante. Even if they don't mention it, everyone knows that children are the best judges of character. There has to be a reason a four-year-old likes you."

"I don't feel right using Frankie that way," Willow says, turning to me worriedly.

I just laugh. "You do know that Auntie Willow/Princess Cinderella is her favorite person on earth at the moment, right? Although she doesn't know what's going on with Dylan, obviously, having us take her to the game while Mommy's away was her idea. I'll just be sick at the last minute."

"Oh. But what if Dylan tries something when we're together and—"

"You don't think you'll actually be alone?" Atlas snorts.

"Jade always has security now," I add. "And Ty will be with

you whenever I'm not. Don't worry about your safety—or Frankie's."

"If I'm honest, I'd like to see Dylan try something with Frankie," Atlas says with a grunt. "Give me an excuse to—"

"Atlas." Madeline gives him a stern look. "Do *not* utter those words aloud. We're in public. Do you understand me?"

"Yeah, yeah." He doesn't finish his thought but the look on his face tells me he's still thinking about it.

Hell, I think of little else these days.

Hurting Dylan and taking care of Willow are the main things on my mind, twenty-four-seven.

"What about my money?" Willow asks after a moment. "At the very least, the money he owes me for the allowance I never got?"

"I just hired a forensic accountant." Madeline smiles, and it might be the most wicked thing I've ever seen. "He's going to rue the day he ever took a dime he wasn't entitled to."

TWENTY-SIX

Willow

I'VE SEEN a lot of green rooms in my life, but Lily Maxwell's is something special.

Or maybe that's the woman herself, tall and beautiful, joy in what she's doing shining out of every single pore. Just being in her presence makes me want to do a pop star biopic in an attempt to capture some of that...*verve.*

"You okay?" Hudson asks, his arm sliding around my waist, drawing me into his side.

"I'm great," I say, smiling up at him, my heart thudding in my chest at the soft way he stares down at me.

He strokes the backs of his knuckles of his free hand over my cheek. "Good, princess."

"Are *you* okay?"

"I'm here with you. How can I be anything but?"

My lips curve and I lift on tiptoe, press my lips to his. "Thank you for coming with me."

"Any—"

"Willow!" I drop back to my heels, head whipping toward Lily, who's waving at me enthusiastically. I only met her before the show and she's already befriended me. Kind of like the rest of Hudson's family.

I want to stay right where I am, standing in Hudson's arms, enjoying the upbeat mood of the room, safe and secure and not worried about whatever the hell it is that Dylan's pulling today.

I want to just be a girl at a concert.

But Lily has been awesome, arranging for the backstage passes, welcoming me even though she's hard at work putting on a show.

My politeness rears its not-so-ugly head. "I should go over and thank her."

His expression is gentle. "Go," he encourages, jerking his head toward Lily. The girls are gathering around her, and she's pulling out her phone for a selfie.

I hurry over and Briar lifts an arm, tugging me into her side as we all huddle up for the picture.

"You all are freaking gorgeous!" Lily exclaims, snapping a few more shots and then holding her phone up so we can scroll through the pictures.

"She's not wrong. We're hot," Briar agrees.

Jade's cheeks go pink, but she bumps her shoulder against mine. "Yeah," she says. "I don't think we're doing too bad at all."

"Not sure this bump can be considered hot," Aspen quips. "But you guys are killing it."

"We're all beautiful," Lily says more firmly, glancing at Aspen for permission before gently settling her hand on Aspen's belly. "But most especially this little bump."

"Yup, puking my guts up, stressing out my fiancé, and wanting to sleep for eighteen hours a day"—Aspen's voice is dry—"totally beautiful."

Jade takes her hand. "You're growing a life, honey, that's beautiful."

"Did I forget to mention the puking?"

My lips turn up as Briar chuckles.

"Rude," Aspen says, jabbing a finger in her direction.

"If we can't laugh at our misery then what hope do we have?"

"The hope to not puke?" Her expression is so intent that I can't help but giggle.

Then blush when four female gazes turn my way. "Sorry," I say, my cheeks heating further. "It's just that you guys are really funny."

Briar blows on her knuckles and buffs them on her shoulder. "Damn right we are."

"And beautiful," Lily says, reaching for my hand and squeezing it. "And really, *really* strong."

The backs of my eyes burn, and I inhale shakily. "Lily... You don't have to say—"

"Anything I don't mean?" Her fingers wrap tightly around mine. "I do. Because I mean it. I've wanted to meet you for ages, even more so since Jade mentioned how wonderful you are."

My lungs spasm again.

How are these women so nice?

Women aren't nice. Or at least the women I know in Hollywood aren't nice. If they can't get something from me—a story to share with the tabloids, a shopping trip for me to pay for, a dinner for them to be seen at—then they don't want to spend time with me.

I'm just a vessel to be used.

But not by *these* women.

They've already done so much for me and they don't really know me.

"Why are you guys so awesome?"

"Ah," Briar bumps my shoulder again and she's grinning, her tone deliberately light. Something I'm thankful for when she says, "We've got you fooled. Sooner or later, the shine will wear off."

Aspen gasps. "Rude."

Lily scowls. "Seriously. *Rude.*"

Even Jade glowers. "No more backstage passes for you."

We all fall silent for a beat.

Then we start laughing.

And it's...perfect. So perfect I feel my eyes welling up again. I wave a hand in front of my face and deliberately blink them back.

Something Hudson notices—because of course he does—and he takes a step toward me, concern written into the lines of his face.

I slap on a smile, wave him away. "I'm good," I mouth.

But that doesn't make the concern disappear.

He starts striding over.

Briar, as intuitive as her brother, steps to my side and wraps an arm around my shoulders. "Shoo!" she calls. "Your *girlfriend*"—she draws the word out with all sorts of sisterly teasing —"is fine. I promise."

His eyes come to mine.

"I *am* fine." This time my smile is real. "It's a girl thing."

"We pinky promise," Aspen says.

"No boys allowed!" Lily calls.

Hudson holds my stare for a long moment. Then half of his mouth turns up and he nods, turning back to the huddle of men on the far side of the room.

"Speaking of boys," Lily says. "Or, I guess, I should say, speaking of *men*"—she jerks her chin toward Atlas, wearing a form-fitting pair of trousers and a crisp white button down with the sleeves rolled up to reveal a set of strong, tanned forearms—"will someone clue me in to who that tall drink of hot broody male is?"

I can't deny that Atlas *is* hot, especially having shucked his jacket and tie.

The man can pull off a suit.

But the slightly disheveled businessman is even hotter.

Still, I'm partial to tight tees and jeans myself. Especially when they're filled out by a sweet and sexy bodyguard with soulful hazel eyes.

"*That* grumpy, broody billionaire is Atlas Delarosa," Briar says, her eyes sparkling with humor. "My boss."

Lily sighs. "Your boss?"

Briar nods.

"Damn," she says. "All the hot ones are off-limits."

Mischief slides across Briar's face. "Not at all." She leans in, stage whispers, "He looks grumpy but he's really a softy beneath that ill-tempered exterior."

I can attest to that.

But before I can say that, Briar's mischief takes hold.

"Boys!" she calls. "Time for a group photo!" And when they don't move, she adds, "Chop! Chop!"

As they are often wont to do, they follow Briar's orders. Moments later we're gathered up for a group photo, Lily and Atlas conveniently positioned next to each other.

"Atlas," Briar says after the snap is complete, "this is Lily. Lily. Atlas."

"She's devious," Hudson murmurs in my ear (after having done some convenient positioning of his own—to end up by my side).

"She's your sister."

He grins down at me. "Ask me how I know."

I giggle and he gently touches my cheek. I lean into him,

loving the soft caress, wanting more, wanting everything he'll give me.

But before I can get lost in that...Atlas has my mouth falling open in shock.

Because the confident businessman seems to be starstruck.

"Atlas"—he lifts his hand for her to shake—"I'm Lily—" She giggles and he jerks his head, as though shaking himself, trying to save the introduction gone wrong. "Lily," he corrects. "I'm Atlas."

She places her hand in Atlas's, lifts up on tiptoe to press her lips to one of his cheeks then the other. "Lovely to meet you, Atlas." She drops back to her heels, winking playfully at him. But when she opens her mouth to say something else, her assistant comes over with a question, and the moment is broken.

Yet I can't help but notice that when she excuses herself and slips away, Atlas's gaze is locked onto her.

I glance at Briar, my eyebrows lifted in question.

Is she seeing what I'm seeing? Confident, albeit slightly distant Atlas with the heart of gold, is stammering over a woman, unable to tear his eyes from her?

Hmm.

Briar's expression tells me she's cottoned on too. She's calculating. *Plotting.*

And when I glance at Jade and Aspen, I see they're wearing similar looks.

Atlas better watch out.

The Gamebreaker ladies are on the matchmaking case.

And I have the feeling he's not going to know what hit him.

TWENTY-SEVEN

Dash

WE'RE BABYSITTING for Frankie tonight since Briar is out of town and Royal and Jade have other plans. It's interesting to look at the world through her eyes, and I have to admit I love watching Willow and her together. Frankie is sweet and adorable and sassy, and Willow sasses her right back, but it's more than that. She's stepped into the role of auntie seamlessly, like she's always been part of us, and it makes me realize just how deep my feelings for her run.

Willow is going to make a wonderful mother someday.

And I can't help but wonder if that's going to be our future. If we are going to build that kind of life—and family—together.

Is it even possible?

We haven't been together very long, but I can't imagine my life without her now that we've met. Can't imagine going back to an existence that doesn't include waking up next to her every day. Laughing with her over dinner. Falling asleep with her in my arms.

"Uncle Dash?" Frankie looks up at me sleepily.

"Yeah, honey?"

"I love you."

My heart melts every damn time she says something like that. I lean over and brush my lips across her forehead. "I love you too, tater tot."

"Good night, sweetie." Willow leans down and kisses the top of her head. "See you in the morning."

"Waffles for breakfast?" Frankie mumbles, her eyes closing.

"Whatever you want."

Willow smiles as Frankie pulls her stuffed hippopotamus closer, nestling deeper into the mattress, and we slip out of the room.

"She's so sweet," Willow says. "I adore her."

"Same." I follow her into our bedroom and we settle on the mattress. She moves into my arms naturally, like she's been doing it her whole life. Like we've been doing this, being a couple, for a lot longer than the two months we've been together.

"Do you want kids?" she asks quietly. "Like, someday?"

"I do," I admit. "I never really had a time frame or number in mind—I just figured it would happen once I met the right woman." I pause. "What about you? Do you see kids in your future?"

"To be honest, I never really thought about it. Then Dylan made the announcement he was ready to get me pregnant." She shudders a little. "And I realized that I absolutely couldn't have kids with *him.* Before that, it was this weird, vague hypothetical. I didn't think pregnancy or childbirth sounded like fun, didn't know if I had it in me to be a good mother, stuff like that. But now..." She hesitates, as if she's struggling with whatever it is she wants to say.

"Now?" I encourage gently.

"Now... I think I do. Spending time with Frankie and seeing how excited Aspen is despite how sick she's been—it's a totally different outlook. And honestly, I'm beginning to see that everything changes once you meet...the right person."

I fucking love hearing that.

"I agree," I say. "Like I said, I figured I'd have them someday but I couldn't be more specific because I knew it would only happen under the right circumstances. And I want to be better than our parents were." I pause. "I mean, they're good people. Briar and I had everything we needed, and they love us, but they're not the most affectionate. They're not interested in family get-togethers, dinners, holidays—they're kind of hands off. I mean, they only see Frankie twice a year."

She blinks. "Really? Their only grandchild and they only see her twice a year? How is that possible?"

"They're semi-retired now so they travel a lot and just do their own thing. It's not that they wouldn't come if we needed them, but I know they were frustrated that Briar had a baby with no father in the picture. And they didn't want me to join the military. I think maybe... we disappointed them."

She stares, a look of distaste on her face. "I don't think I'm going to like your parents. They sound judgmental and icky."

I chuckle. "They're a bit judgmental, for sure. And it's not black and white. It's not like they kicked Briar out or anything. They were just...disappointed. Where you could see it in their eyes. And you know Briar—she doesn't put up with that shit. She works incredibly hard to make sure she never, ever asks them for anything. Not even love for her daughter. Which is the sad part."

"So she created a family of her own with people who give their love freely—people she doesn't have to ask for anything from. They just give it."

"Yeah. They're not bad people, just not the parents we wish they were."

"That's their loss then," she whispers, scooting closer to me. "You're amazing, and the family you've created with your friends and sister—that's special. Something most people would do anything to have. I'm so honored and humbled to even be a tiny part of it."

"Thank you." I kiss the tip of her nose.

"Now it makes more sense why Briar is so intent on Sunday Dinners and is so protective of your family."

"Yeah. I think our upbringing bothers her more than me because... well, I'm a guy. I'm good with a frozen pizza in front of the TV on a Sunday night. She's the one who made me—all of us really—want a more traditional family. The friendship between us guys happened organically, but when Briar had Frankie, she was determined to give her child the life we didn't have. Even if it was subconscious at first."

"That makes sense. I don't recall having a family life, to be honest," she says after a moment. "I have no memories of my father, and then my mom threw herself into making me a star. There were no Sunday dinners, or intimate family get-togethers, or fun holiday trips. It was all work and diets and casting calls and photo shoots."

"That doesn't sound like a great childhood," I say gently.

"No." She shakes her head, her eyes shrouded, as if she's somewhere far away. "I just hate that I can't remember my dad but I can...watch him die."

"What?" I frown in confusion. "What do you mean?"

"He's one of the people who jumped. He was a fireman, but according to his best friend, he found a pregnant woman on the stairs. She was scared and didn't want to burn to death—she wanted it to be over quickly. He did everything to get her and some of the others out, but when they realized there was nowhere to go... they jumped together. There's footage. My mom used to watch it when I was a kid."

"Jesus." I hiss out a breath. "That's fucked up. I'm so sorry, baby."

"He was in contact with the rest of his battalion. His last words were 'tell my girls I love them.' And then he was gone." She swipes at a tear and I tighten my arms around her.

What the hell is wrong with some people? Why would anyone traumatize a child like that? It's different for her mom—she was married to the man and had to deal with the reality of his death. But Willow never knew him.

I really want to shake her mother.

"You want to see his picture?" she asks after a moment.

"Sure." I nod, hoping that brings her comfort.

She slides off the bed and goes to the box of her father's things. She keeps it in the closet, so I can't see it, but I know that's where she's going. I hear her rustling, then some muttering, and finally a curse.

"What's wrong?" I ask, getting up and padding to the closet where she has a murderous look on her face.

"He took it," she hisses. "That bastard took it!"

"A picture of your dad?"

"The picture I put in a little silver frame. He's in his fireman's uniform, holding me. It's the only picture I have of us together." She puts her hands on her hips. "It's my favorite, and he knows it." Her eyes close, more tears sliding free. "We have to go back."

"Babe." I approach her slowly and put my hands on her shoulders. "Short of breaking and entering, you know we can't. You have to be patient."

"It's theft!" she protests, her eyes flying open and searching my face. "It's the one damn thing I have of him and I together. He knows it means the world to me—that's why he pulled it out. He knew there was a chance I'd get my personal things back, so he took the one thing that would hurt me most."

"I know. And we'll get it back, but we need to be patient while Madeline and Atlas work on things behind the scenes."

"What if he destroys it?" she whispers.

The pain in her eyes breaks my heart.

"Someone, somewhere, must have a copy. The negatives. Whatever. I promise you, Willow—if he did destroy it, I will move heaven and earth to get you another copy."

At that, she falls into my arms.

"Thank you," she whispers softly.

Is it wrong that I want to tell her I love her?

That she's the part of me I didn't know was missing?

That I want to give her the world and never let go?

Those kinds of words don't come easy to me.

It's probably too soon anyway.

I don't want to scare her away. She already had both a mother and a man controlling her—what she needs from me is freedom. A man who'll let her find her own way for once.

So that's what I'm going to try to give her.

TWENTY-EIGHT

Willow

THE BEST PART of the last week was making waffles with Frankie and then dousing them in copious amounts of whipped cream and chocolate spread.

Then eating them, I suppose.

Because Frankie had gotten a whipped cream and chocolate mustache and Hudson had wiped it, oh so gently, off her upper lip.

Of course, that was after he'd done something that made me topple a little bit more in love with him—he'd given himself his own mustache. And Frankie's resultant peals of laughter had sent me toppling head over heels for her too.

And then join in on the fun—with the laughter *and* the mustache.

Eventually, though, Briar returned from her business trip and reclaimed her daughter.

And Hudson continued his slow and measured return to

work—mostly in the office, coordinating his men, but also some light protection detail in the field with his favorite long-time clients.

And me?

I'm still in his house.

Still waiting around for Atlas and Madeline to do their work.

Still relying on other people to make it safe for me to live my fucking life.

I grind my teeth together and try to shove down my frustration. I manage it, but it's getting harder with each day that passes—hell with each hour and minute that pass. Because something needs to change. Because I need to figure out how to fill my days with anything that isn't sitting around reading or learning to cook or exercising to continue getting my strength back.

All of those are good.

Productive.

But they're not fulfilling me in any meaningful way.

I'm desperate to dig my teeth into a script, to fall into the study of a new character, to learn and train and become someone else—a single mom trying her best to provide for her kids, a superhero flying through space, the president, a morally gray heroine who isn't afraid to kill for those under her protection.

Hell, I'd even take a sequel direct-to-streaming movie reuniting me with my childhood castmates.

And that would, quite literally, be hell.

But it would be better than this puttering around, day after day, searching for something meaningful, for a way to be useful, for—

"Ugh!" I snap, dropping the mixing bowl into the sink and

flicking on the water, rinsing out the remainder of the banana bread batter.

There are four loaves already.

That's more than Hudson and I can eat, and though he's been taking the leftovers of my baking endeavors to work, I'm sure the guys are going to get sick of the treats eventually.

Or maybe I'm just feeling grumpy.

Okay, maybe it's both.

"Ugh," I mutter again, cleaning the bowl and setting it on a towel on the counter to dry. The bread is in the oven, the dishes are done, I've done my three miles on the treadmill, lifted tiny dumbbells—at least compared to the gargantuan ones that Hudson uses—in a series of exercises that my physical therapist recommended, and tried out a new recipe I found on Pinterest.

Such a full day.

Such a full life.

Ugh.

I clamp my teeth together so tightly a bolt of pain shoots through my jaw, and stand there, just breathing, for long minutes—

For so long, in fact, that the timer for the banana bread goes.

I shake myself, pull out the loaves and leave them to cool then turn off the oven and do the only thing I can do.

Escape.

To the only place I *can* escape.

Hudson's back yard.

The sun is shining and it's a beautiful, sunshiney California day. Blue skies, not a cloud in sight. The breeze ruffles my hair but doesn't chill—chilly isn't something SoCal is known for. Hell, we get a quarter of an inch of rain and suddenly, it's like people's cars don't work any longer.

Commutes get longer.

Traffic gets...traffickier.

Road rage gets...well, *ragier*.

But right now, I wish it was raining. Downpouring. Hailing. Dumping unusual and record-breaking snow on me. Anything except for the bright and cheerful sunshine that is the antithesis of my dour mood.

Spoiler alert: I don't get my wish.

The sun slowly travels across the sky, the day warms even more, and...my mood doesn't change.

I should have looked for the picture before I left Dylan's and my house.

I *should* have.

And now not only am I anchorless, without a path forward, I'm also stuck in this holding pattern, imagining the silver frame dented and dirtied, the glass cracked, small shards escaping and tumbling to the floor, the picture of my dad and I scratched, damaged, or worse...

Torn into a million pieces.

I know I'm being ridiculous. It's just a picture and I have no control over its fate, over what Dylan has decided to do to it. Further that, the image is mine, committed to memory, held deep in my heart.

He can destroy it and I'd still have the memory. Because he can take a lot of things from me—has taken almost everything—but I'm still here.

Still breathing.

Still living—

"Ugh," I mutter again.

Because is that what this is?

Locked in a tower, hiding from the world, from Dylan, from the press. Sitting here and doing nothing while other people move heaven and earth for me.

Ugh!

I pace through the back yard, around the pool, resisting the urge to kick at one of the loungers when my angry, unaware strides bring me in contact with it. But that will only hurt my foot.

The way my luck is going, I'll likely break a toe, and then where will I be?

But even though I resist the urge to do that kicking, my anger doesn't fade. I'm just...so damned angry, as though a lifetime of frustrations is threatening to burst free at any moment. Shoved down time and again, so hard that I forgot it existed.

And now...

It's like I can't keep the lid on it.

Like the rage is boiling up and over and—

My pacing is abruptly halted by a tree branch catching my hair, yanking me to a halt.

"Ow!" I growl, wrenching a hand through my hair to free it and kicking out at the offending tree's trunk. "*Ugh!*" I yell, kicking at it again. "UGH!"

"I'm impressed by the power of your kicks, princess," I hear, "but want to clue me in as to what the poor, innocent tree did to you?"

I still, red-hot embarrassment scorching through me.

Hudson's hand settles lightly on my shoulder, carefully turning me toward him. He crouches a little, his gaze holding mine, and then he proves how wonderful he is because he doesn't hesitate to pull me into his arms, hugging me tight.

The man gives the *best* hugs.

"I'm sorry," I whisper long moments later.

"For what?" he whispers back.

"For being angry for no reason."

He leans away from me, one big hand lifting and cupping

my jaw. "You absolutely have a reason—*reasons*—to be angry, princess. And I'm glad you're letting it out now."

"It's like I have this well of rage in me," I whisper. "One that's been shoved down again and again and *again*." I close my eyes, exhale. "I'm alive and safe and privileged. I shouldn't be angry, especially when so many people are working to help me."

He tucks a strand of hair behind my ear. "You don't have to justify yourself. You've been through hell, been taken advantage of, and you're stuck here in a holding pattern until things shake out. *Of course* you're upset. And I like that you're angry—that tells me you're finally starting to process all the things you've been through, the bad shit that's been done to you. Because any normal person would be pissed, baby. Not just accepting."

I release a shaky breath.

"So let that rage come, let that anger loose. Don't keep it locked inside where it's just going to continue to eat at you."

"It scares me," I admit.

"We'll take it on together."

No hesitation. Not in his words. Not in his eyes.

Just laid out there, same as I know, without a doubt, that he would lay down his life for me.

I love him.

The thought doesn't bring fear to my heart—and likely, it should. But it doesn't.

Because it's just...a forgone conclusion.

So, I don't pull back.

I melt against him, wrap my arms around him in turn, and sigh softly, soaking him in. "Thank you," I murmur.

He pulls back, cups my jaw again. "No thanks needed. Not ever," he adds when I start to protest.

"Stubborn."

His mouth kicks up. "Of course I am. Now"—he jerks his head toward the back door—"want to get out of here?"

I blink. "Out of where?"

"The house."

Another blink. "I thought I couldn't—"

He grins. "Actually," he says. "I just realized I have the perfect place."

TWENTY-NINE

Dash

FOR A RANDOM THURSDAY NIGHT, The Sapphire Room is hopping. The parking lot is full and when we walk in, there are two bartenders handling the crowd—including Aspen. She's taken a huge step back because of her pregnancy, but apparently she's helping out tonight.

I frown a little, because I know Banks won't be happy about it, but he's at the end of the bar drinking a beer and talking to a couple of his teammates from the Vipers, West McGregor and Magnus Forsberg.

"This is your club?" Willow asks, leaning into my side.

"Welcome to The Sapphire Room." I grin at her as we make our way over to Banks.

"Hey!" He looks up with a smile and reaches out to shake my hand. "What are you guys doing here?"

"We needed to get out of the house," I reply.

"*I* needed to get out of the house," Willow adds dryly.

"Welcome." Banks motions to his friends. "This is West

McGregor and Magnus Karlsson. Guys, you know Dash—and this is his girlfriend, Willow."

I see West's brows rise just a tiny bit but then he seems to catch himself and smiles. "Nice to meet you. My mom is a huge fan."

"Tell her thank you," Willow says graciously. "I'm a big fan of yours as well."

Great.

I keep forgetting she's a Vipers fan, and the way she smiles at West makes me want to hit things.

"Fan of what?" Magnus interrupts in confusion.

"This is Willow *St. Claire*," I say, thinking that will clear things up, but the Swedish winger only seems more confused.

"I'm an actress," Willow stage whispers. "But don't tell anyone."

"Oh!" That makes him smile and he shakes her hand. "Then probably my mother is a fan also—she loves American TV."

They start talking about television shows and hockey, Willow completely at ease with two guys she doesn't even know, and I feel a twinge of guilt. I know it's for her safety while we sort out the Dylan mess, but I've basically kept her locked in a gilded cage.

And Willow is a beautiful bird who needs to fly free.

"...you don't *look* like you're in the middle of a nervous breakdown."

I whirl, ready to tell West to shut his mouth but my beautiful exotic bird seems ready, willing, and able to take care of herself.

"Well, you know how it is with exes who don't want to let go." She shrugs. "I've hired an attorney, and she's working on getting him to leave me alone. And to stop talking shit about me. It's getting really *old*."

West nods. "Just let me know if you need a few of us to rough him up."

I snort but cover my mouth and pretend it was a cough.

I definitely don't need guys from the Vipers protecting my girl, but I also don't need her to think I'm some overprotective Neanderthal. She had enough of that with Dylan.

And apparently, she's perfectly capable of handling herself because she barely misses a beat as she disarms West and redirects the conversation.

I love watching her come out of her shell.

"It looks like Aspen is feeling better," I say to Banks, forcing myself to allow Willow the freedom to do her own thing, no matter how hard it is to let go. I'm not the kind of man who's generally overly possessive, but my need to protect her reared its head the moment I saw her in that hospital bed and now that she's mine, I can't seem to let go.

Not that anyone will hurt her *here.*

Certainly not our friends from the Vipers.

"She is," Banks agrees, following my gaze as I watch Willow talking and laughing with West and Magnus. "And we got slammed tonight, so of course she jumped in to help. It's good, though, because she was starting to go stir crazy at home."

"I know how that is. Willow's the same way. I just don't know how to protect her until we get past this bullshit with Dylan."

He nods. "Yeah. He needs to fuck all the way off."

Willow throws back her head and laughs at something West says and I feel a tug of jealousy in my gut that I can't tamp down.

Dammit.

"Relax," Banks says quietly. "She's not interested in *him.*"

"I. Know." I grind out the words even though I don't quite believe them.

Well, my brain does but my heart is an insecure, immature jerk.

"What can I get you guys?" Aspen comes over to us with a smile.

Her belly seems to have doubled in size since I last saw her, and I can't believe Banks isn't losing his mind with her behind the bar, but he's smiling.

"Gamebreaker for me," I say.

"Me too!" Willow calls out, grinning at me. I've told her all about the drink that Colt came up with in college and I know she's anxious to try it.

The ladies chat while Aspen whips up our drinks.

"There you go." She wipes her hands. "And now I'm going to take a break."

Banks immediately reaches for her hand, and I slide an arm around Willow's waist. "Do you want to sit with the others?" I motion to where Briar, Atlas, Royal, and Jade are sitting.

"Of course. Do you want to join us?" she asks West and Magnus before I can stop her.

"Sure." They follow us to our table and pull up extra chairs.

My teeth are on edge as West sinks down next to Willow, but I'm surprised when she turns and presses her lips to mine.

"Jealous much?" she whispers in a teasing voice.

Good thing I'm not *obvious*.

I grunt. "Maybe."

"Don't be. From a romantic perspective, all I see is you. But I'm allowed to have friends, right?"

Well, that takes the wind right out of my sails.

"Absolutely." I stroke her cheek. "Don't mind me. It's been a minute since I had a girlfriend, and after everything Dylan has done, my knee-jerk reaction to everything and everyone is to protect you."

"I know." She smiles, her eyes soft and loving. "And I love it ninety-nine percent of the time. But please let me be who I am, because at my core, I'm social."

"Do your thing, baby."

She winks and turns back to West. "I need to know exactly what you were thinking when you scored that goal against Toronto last week..."

They're back to talking hockey, and suddenly I'm not jealous anymore.

She needs this to be happy, and knowing she's happy is pretty much all *I* need.

I drop my arm over the back of her chair and watch as she talks and laughs with everyone. She's one of us now, and it's a beautiful thing.

I honestly didn't believe the woman of my dreams existed, much less that she would be in the form of a beautiful and delicate movie star with a troubled past. Yet here she is, filling my life and giving me new reasons to wake up every morning.

After we lost Colt, one of the things that got me out of bed was knowing Frankie was on the way. Once she was born, she breathed new life into all of us, and while we still missed him, it started to get easier knowing there was this innocent little girl who needed us to focus our love and attention on her.

There's going to be another baby in the mix soon, along with Aspen, Jade, and now Willow. It almost feels like we're complete, like we've almost moved on from the trauma of losing Colt.

Almost.

Atlas won't be an easy nut to crack.

I wasn't sure there was a woman out there that was right for me, but I can't imagine the type of woman who'll put up with Atlas's bullshit. If it wasn't for us—our family—he would probably have no one in his life.

He has a ton of business associates, acquaintances, and

women who want to sleep with him, but he doesn't have... *friends*. It's been like that since college. We had to drag him into our group kicking and screaming, but hockey forges bonds that would otherwise seem impossible. In retrospect, I can see how he needed us to adopt him, even though he would probably die before admitting it.

And very little has changed over the years.

He's richer and more successful than the rest of us, but he's lonelier than we are too. Again, something he'll never admit, but I worry about him. Especially now that we're all pairing up. I can't help but wonder if there's something between him and Briar. As her brother, that freaks me out, but as someone who cares about her, I'm not so selfish that I want her to be alone.

She needs someone to love her, be a full-time dad to Frankie, and give her the family she's always dreamed of. Yes, we're family, and that will never change, but I want her to have what Willow and I have. What Banks and Aspen have. And I worry that if there *is* something between Briar and Atlas, they're afraid to act on it because of some misplaced fear that I —and the rest of the guys—will be upset.

In the past, I would have threatened him within an inch of his life, but Briar isn't a child. She's a grown woman with a daughter, a career, and a home. If Atlas is the man for her, I don't want them to hide it because of me. That would be selfish as fuck.

As far as I know, Briar doesn't date. And as much as I don't want to think about my sister having sex, I know it's not healthy for a beautiful twenty-six-year-old woman to have zero male companionship that isn't her brother or his friends. I need to have this talk with her at some point, but I'll have to broach the subject carefully. Maybe Willow will have some ideas.

"I think I've been recognized," Willow whispers to me, snapping me out of my reverie.

I follow her gaze and see a few people looking at her, surreptitiously snapping pictures.

But that's a good thing.

She's not doing anything wrong, and if they want to post photos of her living her best life, I'm all for it.

"Are you okay with this?" I ask her.

She nods. "I'm great. I'm with my sexy boyfriend, hanging out with friends and making new ones. What else could anyone ask for?"

And just because I know people are watching, I lean over and press my lips to hers.

"Not a damn thing."

Dylan Durand can suck a bag of dicks.

THIRTY

Willow

"I LOVE GAMEBREAKERS," I say, grinning as I flop back on the mattress.

"I think I love you on Gamebreakers too." He winks at me, and my heart flutters. My man is sexy as hell.

And...I just had the best night in, well, for as long as I can remember.

Chatting with West and Magnus, getting all the insider information and fun behind-the-scenes stories. Laughing with Briar, Jade, and Aspen as Briar shared all the insider information about Hudson and the rest of the Gamebreakers. Okay, so it was less just laughing and more *cackling*, especially when Briar told us the story of the first time the guys babysat Frankie.

Which was also the first time that any of them changed a poopy diaper.

It was a chaotic round of gagging, going through an entire package of baby wipes, three outfit changes for Frankie, and ended with a diaper that was put on backward.

How many Gamebreakers does it take to successfully change a newborn's diaper?

Apparently, more than Atlas, Royal, Banks, and Hudson.

That had me laughing so hard my stomach and cheeks hurt, but it wasn't just Briar telling us all the dirty details. She shared stories that filled my heart too.

How Royal held her hand as she pushed Frankie out—because, for a variety of reasons, Hudson, her parents, and the other guys were too far away to make it in time for the birth. Royal was touring with his former band, happened to be in a nearby city and...he was there to wish Frankie her first happy birthday.

So, yeah, it's not a surprise that he, Frankie, and Briar are close.

Atlas wasn't immune to the stories—we both heard about how he stepped in and offered Briar the job as his assistant and how funny it was that the suave businessman was unusually tongue-tied when meeting pop star, Lily Maxwell.

Considering I was there for that initial introduction, I was able to join in on the teasing.

And, yeah, it was just a little banter, but...it felt good.

Like I was an insider.

Like I'm part of something.

A family I've never had before.

Even now, with half of my mind on Hudson as he strips off his clothes and gets ready for bed and the other half going through the evening, the scenes flashing through my mind one-by-one—and not caring that, more than once, I saw phones pointed in my direction—I know that it's beyond special, what Hudson and the others have given me.

I know I'm beyond lucky.

Privileged.

So fucking in love with Hudson and everyone else that all the painful moments from my past are dulled.

Because the past brought me *here.*

Because I appreciate that what I have now is so much more than I thought I would have, even two years ago.

"Here you go, princess," Hudson murmurs.

I blink, realize he's holding out one of his tees...and that he's just sporting a pair of tight black boxer briefs.

I think I have a new favorite outfit of his.

The waistband hangs low on his waist, showing the indents by his hips, leaving his gorgeous body on display. Six neat boxes on his abdomen, pecs that I've cupped and squeezed, strong shoulders, bulging biceps...and something else is bulging too.

The hard length of his erection is tenting the fabric of his underwear.

He wants me, but he won't take me, not until I give him the clear green light.

Because he's a good man.

I smile, allow my gaze to hang there for long moments, appreciating the view, appreciating the pleasure his body brings me, even while knowing it's not just his body—it's his heart. Only then do I continue permitting my eyes to drift down, past that tempting bulge, past the legs of his boxer briefs, stretched taut around his powerful thighs.

"You're hot," I announce.

He jerks. Then his mouth curves up into a sexy smile. "And you're drunk."

I stretch again, lifting my arms over my head, loving when *his* gaze catches on the fabric pulled taut over my breasts. "I'm not drunk," I say, holding tight to one of the metal rails on the headboard.

And getting an idea.

"Princess," he admonishes gently. "I saw how many Gamebreakers you drank."

"I didn't say I was completely sober." I test the metal, letting the idea percolate through my mind, testing it, seeing if the panic wells up.

I wait...and when it doesn't, I grin.

He chuckles, one warm hand settling on my ankle, pulling off one shoe and then the other. "What's that grin for?"

"No reason," I say, flexing my toes, happy to be out of the heels, then lift up when he unbuttons my pants and tugs them down my hips, my ankles, and off my feet. They land soundlessly somewhere behind him.

"That's not a *no reason* grin, baby." He reaches for the hem of my shirt and I sit up, help him pull it over my head.

"No," I say, lying back down, "I suppose it's not."

"Hmm." A kiss to my temple, his nose nuzzling at the hinge of my jaw. "My good girl's thinking naughty things, aren't you?"

I lift one shoulder in a lazy shrug. "Maybe?" I lay back. "Maybe not."

One palm lands on my belly, pushing gently, pressing me back into the bed. "Which means yes," he says humor creeping into his tone, leaning over me. "What sorts of naughty things, baby?"

"Mmm." God, I love it when he kisses my throat, when he drags his tongue lightly over my collar bones, when he tugs at the fabric of my bra, exposing my breasts, suckling at my nipples.

In fact, I love it so much that I almost forget about my naughty thoughts.

At least, until he murmurs, "Tell me."

"What?"

"Tell me what you want, princess." His hand skates down,

tracing over my waist, dipping into my underwear. "I'll give you anything."

I know that.

Which is why I want to give him this.

"I was wondering..."

A brush of his fingers between my thighs, dancing over my clit. I gasp as pleasure ripples through me, don't bristle at his smug tone when he says, "You were wondering what?"

Because that feels good. No, it feels *incredible.*

Still, I gather what feels like herculean strength to say, "I was wondering where your handcuffs were."

His big body goes statue still. "Princess—"

I reach up, cup his jaw. "I'm ready, Hudson. I want..." I nibble at my lip. "Well, I want *that.*"

"I don't need that, baby. I'm fine with what we've been doing."

"I know." I smile at him. "But I was kind of hoping we could do a little more."

Hot hazel eyes. "You sure?"

I nod.

"Okay, baby." He pushes off the bed, disappears from the room for a minute. I wait for any blip of panic, any sense this might be wrong or too much.

But all I am is certain.

And turned on.

I want to erase that dark memory, want to replace it with something beautiful—because I know that Hudson will give it to me.

He pulls the handcuffs out of the holder and I gulp at the rings of silver. "You sure?" he asks again, putting one knee into the bed.

"I'm *very* sure."

A wicked grin. "Definitely loving these naughty thoughts,

but—" He moves in a rush, rolling to his back, head hitting the pillow next to me.

Before I can ask what he's doing, I hear—

Click.

I gape at him.

Because it's not me handcuffed to the bed frame.

It's...*him.*

"Wh—"

He uses his free hand to cup my jaw. "Someday I'll do that for you"—he presses a finger to my lips when I open my mouth to protest—"Tonight I need you to let me give you this."

My heart pulses.

God, I love him.

And I love him when he orders, "Now climb on, princess, and take anything you want."

Grinning, heart pounding, desire pooling between my legs, I crawl over him.

And I follow those orders to a T.

THIRTY-ONE

Dash

WAKING up with Willow nestled in the crook of my shoulder never gets old. In past sexual encounters, I rarely spent the night, but if I did, I never, *ever* did the whole cuddling thing.

Now I can't seem to do anything else.

When I'm with Willow, all the rules of my life go right out the window.

Willow makes me want to break all my rules—and I fucking love it.

I love *her*.

I haven't used those words in the way they're meant to be used with a woman since... well, a long time. Maybe never. And I still haven't.

But I don't know how much longer I can hold back, or why I'd even want to.

She quickly has become my everything, so I can't think of a single reason why I wouldn't tell her how I feel. Let her know

I'm in this for the long haul. She's had so much uncertainty in her life, I want her to know she can count on me. Always.

"Why are you trying to suffocate me?" she whispers sleepily.

I startle, realize my grip on her has tightened exponentially, and I gentle it without letting go completely.

"Sorry, baby. I was just thinking about how much I love waking up with you... how much I...love you."

"Do you?" There's a catch in her voice and I grip her chin between my thumb and forefinger, urging her to look at me.

"I do. I think I fell a little in love with you the first time I saw you lying there in that hospital bed. I was a goner once I got to know you...and once I touched you? There was no doubt you were going to be mine." I pause. "Unless you don't want to be."

To my surprise, she rolls over and pushes me to my back, straddling me.

"Being yours is the best thing I could possibly be," she whispers, dropping her lips to mine, whispering, "In fact, it's *all* I want to be right now because I love you too. So much I feel like I have to pinch myself sometimes to make sure you—and what we have together—is real."

"I'm real, baby. And what we have is very, very real."

I slide my arms around her and kiss her as lovingly as I know how.

Our tongues twist and twirl, vying for dominance, and her gorgeous body molds to mine. Exactly as it should. Last night's lovemaking was above and beyond anything we've done before and I'm looking forward to doing it again. And again.

Hopefully right now.

Except my phone is buzzing on my nightstand.

Once.

Twice.

Four times.

Talk about cock blocking.

"I may need to get that," I whisper finally. "It's a weekday morning—it might be work."

She nods. "Of course. Do what you have to do."

I grab my phone and frown.

ATLAS: Call me.

ATLAS: Are you sleeping? Fucking call me!

ATLAS: Dude, where the hell are you? I have news that can't wait, and I'm about to get on a plane!

ATLAS: Jesus fucking Christ. Don't make me come over there...

"Atlas apparently has news," I say, dialing his number and putting it on speaker.

"About fucking time," he rumbles by way of greeting.

"You're on speaker," I tell him. "Willow's with me."

"Perfect. Good morning, Willow." He's polite, if not curt. " I have news that's undoubtedly going to make your day."

Our eyes lock for a minute before she says, "Okay. What's going on?"

"Dylan has twenty-four hours to put your allowance for..." We can hear the rustle of papers. "...the last eighteen months in the account of your choice or face contempt charges. Since I don't know what your current banking situation is, I gave them one of my account numbers, but I'll transfer the money to you as soon as you open a new account. Dash knows I'm good for it."

"Oh, my God." She seems frozen, and then she squeezes her eyes shut and tears slip out the sides.

"Baby..." I reach up to wipe them but she shakes her head, smiling.

"I'm fine. I just never thought we'd...win."

"We're also waiting for the warrant allowing the forensic accountant to go through your joint account with a fine tooth comb. There will probably be a lot of money you'll never get back, but there is also a very good chance he'll have to explain and/or return a bunch of it as well. Not to mention, from what we can tell, he used your money for the down payment on the house, so he's going to have to either buy you out or sell it and give you half the profit. The one bit of good news is that your name is on the deed. That was a huge mistake on his part, and we're going to take advantage of it. "

Willow seems shell shocked, staring at the phone open-mouthed.

But she's not crying anymore, which is good.

"I owe you one," I say quietly.

"Nah. We're good." Atlas is rarely warm or sentimental, so his offhand comment is as emotional as he gets.

"Thank you," Willow says after a moment. "I can't tell you how much this means to me."

"We're family," Atlas says gruffly. "And this is what we do for family. You're one of us now. Anyway, I'm on a plane, gotta run. Make sure you set up a bank account so I can get you your money."

With that, he disconnects and I reach for her, putting my hand on the side of her face.

"You okay?"

"I'm more than okay." She takes a long, deep breath and then slowly blows it out. "I'm going to have money again, Hudson. Do you have any idea how important that is?"

"I do."

"And if I get money from the house too, I can buy something of my own."

This seems like the perfect opening for something else I've been thinking about. "What if we bought something of our own... *together*?"

She frowns a little. "You want to move in together? Officially, I mean? Are you sure?"

"Absolutely. Why not? I never want to wake up without you next to me unless one of us is working or there's some kind of emergency. I love having you here with me. What do you think?"

Her eyes twinkle as she nods. "I think it's an amazing idea —I love being here with you too."

"Do you want to live here in my house or should we try to buy something new—a fresh start for both of us?"

"I guess it depends on money," she says, her brows knitting together slightly. "I don't know how much I'm going to have or what my earning power will be going forward. Let's take some time to research what's out there and then decide."

"One day at a time," I say gently. "Let's let Atlas and Madeline work their magic and we'll live here until we get a resolution."

"Okay." She nods thoughtfully, and I can tell by the look on her face she has a lot going on in her head.

"What are you thinking?" I ask.

"I feel like today is the first day of the rest of my life."

"I like hearing that."

"Would you be able to take me to open a bank account today? That feels like one of the first things I need to do so I can move forward."

"Absolutely."

"And then I'm going to start hunting for a new agent. I

need to be able to go back to work at some point. If anyone is willing to take a chance on me." Her face falls a little.

"They will be," I assure her. "Kate is already working on all that bullshit Dylan put online. You're going to have more work than you want."

"What if I don't? What if no one wants to work with me because they believe him?"

"As much as it pains me to say this in this particular context, the truth of the matter is, Hollywood loves a good scandal. No matter what you do or how badly you behave, they're mostly willing to give you a chance just to see what's going to happen. Look at all the celebrities who do genuinely terrible things and then come back with a completely rebranded image? They're going to give you a chance solely so they can have a front row seat to watch you fail. It's fucked up, but it should also give you hope. And once they see how amazing you are—and what a fucking liar Dylan is—you're going to be Hollywood's darling again before you know it."

"The only person's darling I want to be is yours," she whispers.

I reach up to run my fingers through her soft hair. "That's a given," I say softly.

Her eyes flutter closed and she breathes deeply again. "I really love hearing that. I love you, Hudson."

"You have no idea how much *I* love hearing that." I pull her down for another soul-bending kiss. "Now...where were we before we were so rudely interrupted?"

She straddles me again and before I realize what's happening, she sinks down on my cock. "Right here, I think."

THIRTY-TWO

Willow

I SIGN my name with the distinct notion that this is the most important autograph of my life.

We decided that I would pay a lump sum toward the mortgage...okay, well *I* decided that. Hudson was happy to do whatever I wanted—buy a new place together, rent somewhere else to try out a new neighborhood, live in a high rise downtown or the beach in Malibu. But I like it here. It's home, even though I haven't been here long. My safe space.

And somehow *our* space, even though Hudson has lived here for several years.

Which was why he tried to decline my offer of paying toward the mortgage.

But I have a bank account—something we set up the same day that Atlas called several weeks ago to share the good news about my allowance—and I have the funds to contribute.

So, even though I know I triggered his protective side, Hudson let me write that check and cashed it—I checked—

before I would accept being put on the deed. And now...I slide the stack of paperwork we've just finished going through back to the real estate attorney we secured for this job.

June smiles, stows the papers away in a folder. "I'll get these over to the title company and we should have the updated deed in just a few weeks."

Hudson settles his hand on my nape, squeezing lightly.

I glance up at him, mouth curving into a wide smile. "We did it."

He kisses the tip of my nose. "We did."

"I love you," I whisper.

His lips find my ear. "I love you too," he murmurs.

I hear a soft sigh and remember myself. Cheeks heating, I manage to tear my gaze off my man and turn toward the attorney. "Sorry," I say, barely resisting the urge to cover what I know must be blazing red skin.

"Don't be." She shoves the folder into her briefcase. "I'm happy that true love still exists."

Which is a sentiment that doesn't help my hot cheeks, but I can't deny that she's right.

I never knew what true love was...until Hudson.

Until the rest of the Gamebreaker crew.

"I'll walk you out," Hudson murmurs when she stands and starts to gather the rest of her things. "I have to get on the road anyway." He bends back to my ear, words hot, damp puffs that make me shiver. "I'll see you there?"

"I'll be the one with sparkles on."

He straightens, mouth curved. "You and everyone else in the crowd."

He's doing security for Jade's concert tonight and I know the vibe is going to be a celebration. Her music is bright, upbeat, and beyond fun, and her fans seem to make it their personal mission to ensure everyone around them has that same experience.

We'll be in the crowd—well, in a partitioned-off section of the stadium that's surrounded by security.

But...we'll be *in* the crowd.

Not sequestered in a green room, watching through monitors.

Not isolated and on display, expected to act with perfect decorum.

I can let loose, be myself, and have fun with my girlfriends.

I *can't* wait.

"I'll see you tonight," I promise. "In sparkles. And a huge smile on my face knowing that the man I love made it possible."

The gold flecks in his hazel eyes melt, turning soft and sweet, and he leans down, brushes his lips against mine.

But it's only a brief touch because we hear another soft sigh.

"Sorry," June murmurs and I don't like that her eyes look a bit sad. "I'll just..." She hitches a thumb over her shoulder. "Head out." And then she hurries away, heels clicking as she rushes to the front door.

"Go," I order Hudson softly, squeezing his arm before nudging him away. "Make sure she's okay." And when he seems ready to protest, I add, "I need to get ready anyway."

Steady eyes on mine for a long moment.

Then the front door opens and he spurs into action.

He snags his wallet and keys, shoves his phone into his pocket. "Text me when you're on your way, okay?"

"Anything you want, honey."

He's heading for the hall, but that has his gaze flicking over his shoulder, a wicked smirk on his face. "Better be careful saying that, princess. If I remember correctly, it's my turn next to use the cuffs."

Then he disappears, phantom fingers from those silken words stroking between my legs.

It's when I'm zipping up my short, sparkly dress while scrolling through social media that I see the headline.

Pre-production begins in Melbourne for Dylan Durand's latest flick.

My heart skips a beat, but when I go to scroll by—because I've been actively avoiding anything that involves Dylan and/or myself, my brain processes what the words are actually saying.

And what they mean for *me*.

Dylan is in Australia.

And my name is on our house.

And Atlas got the restraining order revoked.

And *Dylan is in Australia.*

Which means he's not here in California and I can legally go into the house and get...my picture.

My heart throbs. If he hasn't destroyed it.

I push that last thought down and look at the time on my phone. I'm almost ready. If I leave in the next couple of minutes, I'll have time to drive out to the house and look for it.

Heart pounding, I stare at my reflection in the mirror.

Determined. Strong. Not a weakling too scared to act.

I nod. I can do this.

I'll grab my picture and get the hell out.

I slick another layer of lipstick on, make sure my earrings are secure, then I grab my purse, Frankie's jacket that I promised to drop by on the way to the concert, and hurry out of the house.

"I can do this," I whisper.

I have time. I'm strong enough.

Dylan's not here.

I snag the key to Hudson's extra car, climb in, and zip down the road.

Luckily, Briar and Frankie don't live far—because L.A. traffic is no joke—so it doesn't take me long to be bounding up their porch, ringing the doorbell, and smiling as Frankie opens the door.

She looks to be in the middle of dinner—her mouth sporting a chocolate milk mustache and Briar's on the phone at the mouth of the hall.

She locks eyes with me, mouths, "Sorry," and I wave her off, holding up Frankie's jacket.

"Thanks," she mouths when I hang it on the coat rack. "No," she says into the phone. "That doesn't work for us..." Her voice grows quieter as she disappears down the hall.

I'm desperate to get to the house, to get my picture.

But...Frankie.

"Do you need help with dinner?" I ask her.

"Nope." She shakes her head, ponytail swinging. "Mom's just..." She scrunches her face up, as though concentrating on her next words and the careful way she says them tells me she's parroting Briar. "Clearing the decks"—a nod that's so damned cute my heart squeezes—"so we have no interruptions for Jade's concert." Her face brightens. "I told her I want to sing and dance along to every song."

My feet throb just thinking about it.

But I still smile and say, "Absolutely," when she asks me to dance with her too.

"Are you going to ride with us?"

"No, sweetheart," I say, smoothing back her hair. "I have to stop by my house for something, but I'll meet you there."

"Uncle Dash's house?"

"My old house." I force a smile. "I need to pick up a picture I left behind."

"A picture?"

"Yeah, sweetie. It's a really special one of me and my dad. But I'll grab it really quick and then we'll dance all night long. Sound good?"

Her lips press flat as she considers that.

Eventually, though, she gives me a sharp nod. "Sounds good."

I fight a smile, jerk my chin in the direction of the kitchen. "Finish your dinner, peanut."

"Okay!" She hugs me tightly then runs off, and I move equally quickly to my car. I need to hurry now. Time is getting short, especially having to drive across town.

Traffic is stop and go, but it still seems like mere heartbeats before I'm pulling into the driveway of the ostentatious mansion, eyes searching for any sign of Dylan and his cronies. But the house is quiet, shut up tight...

Exactly as it would be when we were traveling out of the country for work.

I park, pop open the driver's side door, and then I'm walking up to the house, reaching for the keypad with shaking fingers.

Because this is where this might all go wrong.

If he deactivated my code...

Whir!

The lock disengages and I try the handle, relief pouring through me as I push the door open.

Being here, walking through the entryway, running up the wide staircase to the second floor, hustling down the hall to my old bedroom has fear skittering down my spine, terror clawing through my middle.

I don't like it.

This isn't home—it never was.

But I push those thoughts away, move through the bedroom, and start searching.

First the drawer where my box had been stored in the closet, then the remainder of the space. Then my nightstand and Dylan's. The bathroom. The linen cabinet. The spare bedrooms. The extra bathrooms. Downstairs—the kitchen and mudroom, laundry and pantry, half bath, the library, the family and living rooms, and then…finally…

Dylan's office.

Panic claws up my throat—

I forcefully shove it down and deliberately take a step forward. Then another. Then *another.* Until I'm searching the shelves, the file cabinet, and eventually…his desk.

One drawer.

Another.

Another.

Another.

And then—

Buried beneath a stack of papers…

I see it.

I jerk my hand out and grab the silver-framed picture of my dad and me, and all the air in my lungs rushes out of me.

It's perfect.

It's beautiful.

It's—

"Oh, you dumb, dumb bitch."

THIRTY-THREE

Dash

I'M ten minutes later than I intended—fucking L.A. traffic—but I make my way backstage to meet up with the others. I spot Atlas and almost stumble because...he's not wearing a suit.

He's not wearing a suit?

I can't help but stare in confusion.

Other than our occasional hockey games, where he shows up in sweats, or when we golf, Atlas always wears a suit. Tom Ford is his go-to, though he saves the Armani for special occasions. Even when we hang out at The Sapphire Room and the rest of us are in jeans, he wears a suit. He takes the jacket off and rolls up his sleeves after a few drinks but—I'm having a really hard time with this.

Not only is he not wearing a suit, he's in *jeans*.

They're starched and someone probably ironed them, but he's wearing them.

Along with a Jade Cantrell concert T-shirt.

What's happening here?

"Hey." I walk over to join him and Royal, who are drinking beer.

Atlas also rarely drinks beer, only at the beach or the hockey rink.

"You're late," Royal points out with a smirk.

I flip him the bird. "Some of us *work* for a living."

He rolls his eyes. "Take another ninety-year-old to the doctor today?" He always teases me about my favorite elderly client.

"Better than sitting on my ass all day."

He smirks. "Jealous much?"

"You're late!" Briar comes over to join us.

"Thanks." I look around for Willow, frowning a little when I don't see her. "Willow in the ladies room?"

Briar shakes her head. "No, haven't seen her since she dropped off Frankie's jacket."

I pull out my phone to check for messages but there's nothing from her.

I'm about to text her but then stop myself.

She needs freedom.

L.A. traffic is the worst—and unpredictable—at any time of day. She's probably sitting in it and I'm not going to pull a page out of Dylan's book by demanding to know where she is.

"Hey, everybody." Jade comes out of her dressing room, all dolled up for the show, and I can't help but smile at the way Royal looks at her. Like she's an appetizer, main course, and dessert—all rolled into one.

"Auntie Jade, can we take a selfie?" Frankie asks as she runs up to her. "For my Insta?"

I nearly choke on the beer Banks just put in my hand.

"Her *Insta*?" I ask before I can stop myself.

Frankie giggles. "Mommy let me!"

Briar chuckles. "Don't worry, she only has access to it on my phone, and it's mostly pictures of cats."

"And Auntie Jade." Frankie's eyes beam with delight.

She really loves her aunties, which is pretty cool.

They take pictures while we talk about the Vipers' season, and I surreptitiously keep checking my watch.

"Call her," Atlas murmurs. "You're about to crawl out of your skin."

"I have to let her...be," I say quietly. "I can't constantly check up on her. That's what Dylan did and she needs to be able to... adult."

His brows furrow together. "But—"

"Believe me, I know. But I can't be so overprotective that I potentially drive her away." I take a pull from my beer bottle. "I love her."

Royal's brows nearly reach his hairline and Banks throws back his head and laughs. Atlas simply cocks his head. "So... this is it, huh?"

"She paid off my house and I put her name on the deed this morning, so yeah."

"That was fast," Royal says, letting out a low whistle. "But I get it."

"She needed something of her own, but she wanted it to be half of *my* house. We looked at other properties and nothing felt right to her. Except my place."

Banks grins. "That's awesome."

"Happy for you," Atlas says, nodding.

"Poor Willow," Royal deadpans. "Does she know what she's getting into?"

"Don't make me kick your ass," I mutter. "Can't be worse than what poor Jade has signed on for."

We all laugh, our light-hearted banter distracting me from worry.

But I glance at my watch again.

Then I check my phone.

"She's fine," Aspen says, smiling at me. "Like you said, let her figure out her new normal. Maybe she stopped for a bottle of water or to buy flowers for Jade or whatever. I'm sure there's a perfectly reasonable explanation."

"Traffic," Atlas and Briar say at the same time.

I narrow my eyes at them, about to say something snarky before I remember my suspicion that there might be something between them.

Until Lily walks in, running over to Jade.

They hug and whisper together, obviously talking shop, but it's the way Atlas stares in that direction that gets my attention. He's... fascinated? Infatuated? I don't know how to describe the look on his face. I've never seen it before. Then he guzzles the rest of his beer—something else I haven't seen since college.

Okay, so it's not Briar he's into.

This is a fun twist.

I momentarily feel bad for my sister before realizing she's not even aware, completely immersed in her conversation with Aspen, oblivious to the...lovesick look on Atlas's face?

What the hell?

I almost laugh, but I don't dare. Not only would he kill me, but I wouldn't want to do anything to embarrass Lily. Especially since I don't know if there's something going on there.

I have no qualms about giving Atlas shit, though.

"What's wrong with you?" I demand, elbowing him.

"What are you talking about?" he snaps, scowling.

"Why are you staring at Lily like she's your next meal?"

"Because he's got a hard-on for her," Royal stage whispers. "Duh."

"I do not." Atlas straightens his spine and fixes us all with the same look that tends to make his business competitors quake in their boots.

It's less effective on us.

"It's okay to like a girl," I say pointedly.

"Fuck you," he mutters.

"Does she know you're alive?" Royal asks dryly.

"Oh, she knows," Banks says. "She's just not interested in the moody fucker."

"Fuck *all* the way off," Atlas grunts.

"Good evening, everyone," Lily says, coming over to us with Jade in tow.

"Lily's going to do a song with me tonight," Jade says, sliding her hand into Royal's. "And then Royal will come out to do 'Midnight Snow,' so it'll be a fun night."

"Hey, Lily." I smile at her.

"Hi, Auntie Lily!" Frankie comes running over.

"Hey, there, sugar plum!" Lily reaches down to scoop her up and spin her around.

"Mommy, are you getting this?" Frankie demands when they're done.

"I'm on it," Briar says dryly, holding up her phone to signify she took pictures.

"How's it going, Atlas?" Lily's eyes twinkle as she looks at him, and I realize she knows. She knows he likes her and is teasing him. I'm not sure whether to feel bad for him or if he's getting exactly what he deserves after so many years as the consummate playboy.

Because I'm a thousand percent sure this woman will have no trouble going toe-to-toe with him, whether it's in the bedroom or the boardroom.

"Er, uh...good," he stammers. "How is... uh, how are... you?"

It takes a lot of self-control not to burst out laughing, but as much as we love to give each other shit in private, embarrassing him in front of a woman who isn't part of our inner circle isn't something we do. And anyway, Lily appears perfectly capable of handling herself. And him.

"I'm doing great!" She grins at him. "I don't think I've ever seen you without a suit—I like it."

"Oh." He looks down, as if caught by surprise. "Uh... thanks."

Jesus.

He's got it *bad*.

I've never seen him tongue-tied for any reason, much less in front of us.

He's a grown man, but my buddy obviously needs a little help here.

"When's your next album coming out, Lily?" I ask, opting to change the subject and save Atlas from himself.

"No idea," she says, laughing. "I've been on tour for two years, on and off, and I've written enough songs for two or three albums, but I'm not feeling the urge to go into the studio. For one thing, I get restless, and for another, I make most of my money on tour."

"Meanwhile, I love the studio," Jade says, laughing. "So I can go home to my honey every night."

We all groan and roll our eyes as Royal kisses her.

"Where's Willow?" Lily asks, looking around. "Isn't she coming?"

I realize it's almost showtime and Willow still isn't here.

I check my phone again, but there's nothing.

"I don't think calling to make sure she doesn't have a flat tire or something is hovering," Banks points out after a moment.

I nod and grab my phone, dialing her number.

It rings and rings...and rings.

Until voicemail kicks in and I hear her sweet voice. "This is Willow. You know what to do. Have a great day!"

"Fuck." I disconnect and try not to freak out.

Even if she's stuck in traffic or got a flat tire or something, she should have picked up. She has to know I'm worried.

"She went to get her picture," Frankie chirps when no one says anything.

My blood runs cold.

"Her what?" Briar asks carefully.

"Her picture. At her old house." Frankie cocks her head. "Of her daddy."

Oh my fucking God.

I whirl and start to run.

"Call my team for back-up!" I yell over my shoulder. "I'm heading to Dylan's!"

THIRTY-FOUR

Willow

"OH, YOU DUMB, DUMB BITCH."

I freeze, my fingers clenching on the frame, horror gathering in my belly.

Then I slowly swivel around, ice filling my veins.

He's there. Dylan. And he doesn't look pissed off at me for once.

He's *thrilled.*

Which is maybe the scariest expression I've ever seen on his face.

And I'm abruptly aware of how fucking stupid this is, coming here for a picture. It's important, it holds a giant space in my heart...but I don't *need* it. The snapshot of my dad and me is imprinted in my mind. If Dylan had broken the frame, shredded the photo, I would have still remembered every detail.

His old-fashioned mustache I swear I can remember tickling my hair.

His bright blue eyes that danced with humor and light.

His strong arms holding me tight.

My wide, toothless smile and the pure joy on my face—the evidence of how much I loved and adored him.

My baby fine hair a wild cloud—something I know he did because my mom scoffed at how bad he was at doing my hair... and picking out my clothes.

Because they don't match, the red-striped overalls he put me in and the bright blue T-shirt.

But I don't care.

I had him close and loving on me and—

He was a protector too, looking out for others, sacrificing everything to get people out...until he couldn't.

He wouldn't have wanted me to risk everything for a damned photo.

No matter that it's my only one.

No matter that the frame had sat on his desk at the fire station, clearly important to him too.

He still wouldn't have wanted me in danger to save this.

And neither did Hudson.

God, I should have waited, been patient, ridden this out—just like we had with my money. I let the lawyers and Atlas do their thing and in the end, it had worked out in my favor.

But no, I had to stupidly rush in and—

Dylan takes a step toward me and instinctively, I skitter back, my hip banging against the corner of the desk, sending a sharp bolt of pain through my side.

"Stay away from me." My voice only wobbles the slightest bit.

He smirks as he takes another step toward me and my fingers clench on the frame, but I manage to move more carefully, to sidestep his office chair, to put the length of the desk between us.

I'm nowhere near safe.

But the panic in my belly, coiled tight and ready to strike, stays like that. Not lurching out, not stealing my thoughts and controlling my body.

If I'm calm and smart, maybe I can get a call out to Hudson.

If I'm strong and centered, maybe I can make my way out of the house, can get to my car, can...

"You've really fucked up my life," Dylan says, slowly moving toward me, slowly stalking me around his desk.

I shift my grip on the frame, slip my other hand into my pocket. "The feeling's mutual," I say, and this time there isn't the least bit of waver in my voice.

Something he notices.

Something he doesn't like given the way his sneer grows on his face.

Fuck sneaky.

I take several steps toward the door and pull out my phone. "Just leave me alone, Dylan. All I wanted was my dad's picture. If we're smart, we can handle this quietly and both go on with our own lives."

"Don't you understand by now"—he takes several large steps toward me and the distance I've been so carefully creating between us evaporates—"that you don't give me orders?" He bends, putting his face all of an inch away from mine.

So, I can see his temper ratcheting up.

His control fraying.

Can almost feel his fists connecting with my body.

I've gotten my cell free, and I point it at my face, unlocking the screen. "I'm not trying to give you orders," I say, continuing to back up as I jab at the phone icon, pulling up my recent contacts, finger reaching for Hudson's contact.

I don't make it that far.

Before the pad of my finger can hit his name, my phone is

batted out of my hand. Fingers wrap around my wrist so tightly that I cry out in shock and pain, then again when he roughly twists my arm behind my back and shoves me forward.

Hard.

I hit the built-in bookshelves so hard that I see stars and as my vision clears, I feel something hot sliding down my face.

Blood, I realize.

Dripping from my eye, down my cheek, my jaw...

Dropping onto the pretty, sparkly outfit I was so excited to put on earlier.

Staining it. *Ruining* it.

And I feel it then...my rage. Filling my belly, pulling apart the panic, piece-by-piece, tearing it to such tiny shreds that I don't feel it at all.

The only emotion that's coursing through my veins, burning through my insides...

Is anger.

Red hot *anger*.

Because he ruined my outfit. And tried to ruin my life. And...hell, but he almost managed to ruin *everything*.

My rage bursts out of me, and I fight against his hold on my wrist, his body pressing me into those shelves. I buck and yank, shove and grunt...and the asshole doesn't move an inch. He's so much bigger than me.

So much stronger.

The panic begins to slide back in and—

No!

Every part of my body goes tight—my jaw, my abs, my thighs and calves, and...my fingers.

On the frame of my picture.

Without thinking, I lift my free arm, lift that frame, and I slam it back against Dylan's head.

He shouts in pain, grip on my wrist loosening, and I lurch away from him.

But I barely make it three feet before he's there again, this time tackling me to the floor. I go down hard, the picture flying from my grip with a sickening crunch, the air rushing out of my lungs. Still, even as my head hits the hardwood and stars flash across my vision again, I see that he's bleeding.

Just above his eyebrow.

Like me.

Good.

Barely does that word cross my mind before it all begins to go wrong.

Or rather, it *continues* to go wrong.

Because he wraps his hands around my throat and squeezes. Too hard. Too fast. I can't catch my breath, can't draw in air, can't do anything but claw at his arms, pull at his wrists, trying desperately to get free.

And failing.

Black creeps into the edges of my vision.

My lungs scream.

My arms drop to the floor—

And I feel it.

The metal of the picture frame.

My dad rescuing me a second time.

I scrabble at the frame, fumbling for too long before I manage to grasp it. My arm is heavy and it feels like it weighs a thousand pounds when I lift it.

When I slam it against Dylan's head.

He grunts but continues squeezing.

Again, princess, I hear Hudson say.

I draw back, swing it forward a second time.

Again, baby girl, I hear my dad say.

Dylan curses, and his grip loosens enough that I draw in much-needed air, giving me the strength to swing a third time.

It collides with his temple in a sickening crunch, and I watch in horror as his eyes roll back in his head before he collapses on top of me.

And *that's* when I hear the shouting.

THIRTY-FIVE

Dash

THE PANIC in my chest threatens to consume me.

All I can think about is getting to Willow before it's too late.

I don't care how many laws I break or what the repercussions might be but I don't knock, don't stop, don't think about anything but getting to Willow.

"Willow!" I yell her name as we—Banks, Royal, and Atlas refused to let me come alone—race through the massive foyer, oblivious to the sirens in the background or Atlas's admonishment to "be careful—he might be armed."

Because he knows I'm not.

But it doesn't matter.

I'll die before I let him hurt her.

Not now.

Not ever again.

I hear what sounds like a scuffle and pivot in that direction. The French doors leading to an office are open and I see movement on the floor. Dylan is sprawled on top of Willow, choking her, and my vision blurs red.

"Willow!" I'm poised for a fight but before I can reach them, I see her hand holding something silver—and bashing him repeatedly in the head.

"*Babe.*" This time my voice is a hushed whisper as I pull Dylan off her and she wilts in relief.

Dylan isn't out cold, but he's definitely woozy, blood oozing from multiple wounds on his head.

Jesus, she did a number on him.

Despite everything, I almost smile.

She fought back.

"You all right, Willow?" Banks is kneeling beside her now.

"I-I'm okay... I think." She looks up and...she's bleeding.

She's fucking *bleeding*.

I'm going to end him.

I'm going to make him wish he'd never been born.

I'm going to—Atlas brushes past me and stands over Dylan.

"She's crazy," Dylan rasps, struggling to sit up and holding his head. "She tried to kill me—"

"Stay down." Atlas puts his foot in the middle of Dylan's back.

"I'm pressing charges! Call the cops—Mrs. Wilkes!"

"Shut the fuck up." Atlas looks to me. "Do I need to call Madeline?"

I nod at Atlas then reach for Willow, staring at the blood coating her hand from a gash on her temple. "Where else are you hurt?"

"I...don't know. Here, I guess." She touches her forehead again and then stares at her hand blankly.

"Cops are here," Banks says quietly. "What do you want to do?"

"He was choking me," Willow whispers, her face suddenly pale. "I hit him... with my dad's... picture..."

"I don't know," I respond briskly, "but the first thing I'm doing is taking her to the hospital to get checked out."

"No, I'm okay." Willow tries to protest, but I cut her off.

"You have a deep gash on your forehead, and just a few months ago you got hit in the head so hard you were in a coma," I tell her, trying to keep my voice level. "You need to have a doctor look at you. Don't argue with me about this, please."

Before she can answer, Royal approaches with what looks like a dish towel. "Here—put this on your head."

"Thank you." She shivers suddenly, and I worry she's going into shock.

"Here." I take off the denim jacket I'm wearing and drape it over her shoulders.

"Hudson, I—" she begins.

"Not now," I say gruffly, turning away. I'm battling too many disparate emotions to talk to her right now. I'm pissed off she did something so reckless, but simultaneously thankful she fought back.

Thankful we got here in time.

Thankful she's alive.

I'm also afraid if I try to have a conversation with her, all those emotions are going to burst out of me in an explosion of terror, annoyance, and a plethora of other negativity that I don't think she's ready for. Not from me anyway.

Then the cops burst in and there's a lot of chaos.

Questions.

Dylan playing the victim.

Madeline arriving.

So much fucking chaos.

Luckily, I know these particular officers and have dealt

with them before, so they let me leave with Willow—she's going to the emergency room whether she likes it or not.

And she isn't any happier with me than I am with her at the moment.

"We'll handle everything here," Atlas tells me. "Make sure she gets checked out. Another bump to the head this soon after the coma..."

"I know. Thanks." I turn to Willow. "Let's go."

She blinks at my stern tone but then follows me out without a word.

We're both quiet in the SUV on the way to the hospital.

There's a part of me that wants to grab her hand, hold her, tell her everything is okay, but I don't know if I can. I feel like I'm hanging on by a thread, trying to stay strong for Willow while simultaneously wanting to shake her. I'd never touch her in anger, but I'm so fucking frustrated by what she did.

What was she thinking?

Dylan could have—probably would have—*killed* her.

And for what? A picture that we can almost definitely reproduce at some point?

I can't wrap my head around her risking her life—the life we're building together—for a picture. I understand the sentimental value, but I'm struggling with this. Struggling with her lack of thought—her complete disregard not just for her safety but for how her actions could potentially impact the rest of us.

How it would impact... *me*.

That's probably selfish as fuck, but I've already lived through the nightmare of someone I love being reckless. So reckless he ended up dead. Without me there to have his back. Because he didn't tell me what he was doing.

Why do strangers trust me with their lives but not the people who are fucking closest to me?

It's tearing me up and making my head hurt.

And the worst part is—I have no idea where we go from here.

It's two in the morning before we get home, and I'm still reeling, operating on autopilot. At Dylan's house, at the hospital, when the cops came to get Willow's statement—this is what I do for a living.

But it's different with Willow.

This is the woman I'm in love with, and she took a risk for absolutely no reason, putting me in an untenable position.

Just like Colt.

He never should have re-enlisted without telling me.

I should have been there to have his back on that last mission.

I should have—

"You're mad at me." Her voice interrupts my self-flagellation and I grab a bottle of water out of the fridge, taking a big gulp in an attempt to postpone the inevitable conversation.

The argument I know is coming.

I don't know how to respond because I *am* mad.

In fact, I'm not just mad—I'm fucking furious.

"Hudson? Will you talk to me? Please?" Her voice is soft, eyes filled with regret, and I look into them in frustration.

"I don't know what you want me to say!" I snap, my control slowly beginning to crumble. "What the hell were you thinking?!"

"I just wanted my dad's picture. I—"

"Why?" I throw up my hands, sending a spray of water into the air since I'm still holding the bottle. "How is a picture of a dead man more important than your life?"

"It's the only picture I have of him, dammit!" she yells back, folding her arms across her chest.

"Was it worth it? Was getting his picture worth it when Dylan had his hands around your throat and was choking you? Was it worth the new trauma and scaring the living shit out of me and all our friends?"

"I thought he was in Australia!" she snaps. "I wouldn't have gone if I had any inkling he was still here but—"

"So why didn't you just fucking ask me?" I demand, my voice even louder than before despite my best efforts to keep my temper in check. "I'd do *anything* for you—including breaking the law to send my men in to find it! Why couldn't you just fucking ask me before you went and did something so dangerous?!"

"You're not my father! I'm not going to ask your permission every time I want to leave the house!"

I rear back like she hit me.

That stings.

"That's what you think this is about?" I ask in a steely voice. "After all we've been through, you think this is about asking *permission*?"

We stare at each other for a long moment and something inside of me breaks.

I've bent over backwards to help her heal, find her way out of the darkness, and come out the other side—with me. The last thing I ever want to do is control her.

But if she truly believes that's what I'm trying to do, then everything I've done has been for naught.

And I can't do this.

Not even for someone who literally owns every piece of me.

"Hudson, wait—"

I hear her but I don't look back, don't stop moving.

If I do, I might say something I regret. Something I can't take back.

So I head for the stairs, taking them two at a time until I get to our room. I go straight to the bathroom and turn on the shower. Then I strip out of my clothes and stand under the steaming spray. With my hands against the wall, I let my chin hit my chest and memories ricochet through the windows of my soul.

The fear I felt when I realized she might be alone with Dylan was the most intense emotion I've ever experienced. Losing her was—*is*—unfathomable. There's no universe where I'll ever let anything happen to her, and all she seems worried about is her freedom.

I thought she trusted me.

I thought—*fuck.*

I thought she loved me the way I love her.

THIRTY-SIX

Willow

I WATCH him pound up the stairs and know that I've seriously messed up.

"Dammit," I whisper, clenching my hands into fists, pressing them against my temples.

It's just...

Dylan and all the bullshit he heaped onto me.

And that's not fair.

Not fair to Hudson.

Because he's never been anything like Dylan, not from the first moment he began reading to me. And it's not okay for him to think that I would put him in the same category as my ex, not even for a second.

Because Hudson has done nothing wrong, nothing except care for me and love me and show me what a beautiful life I can have.

A beautiful *family*.

My eyes sting, and I blink rapidly as I try to find center, try to figure out what I can say to make him understand I didn't mean that.

He's been through so much, and he seems tough and impermeable, but he feels deeply.

So, I know I've *hurt* him deeply.

"Shit," I whisper.

I messed up, and not even just with that conversation, but by going to Dylan's house in the first place. Hudson was right—I could have talked to him, could have worked with him to come up with a plan to get my photo back. He would have been right by my side if I insisted.

But I shouldn't have insisted.

Because it's exactly what I thought during those first terrifying moments that Dylan stalked me in his office—my dad loved me, my dad protected people for a living, put himself between them and danger, and...

He wouldn't have wanted me to risk myself for a piece of paper.

No matter how important it is to my heart.

I was dumb.

Reckless.

And...now I owe the man I love an apology.

Even as I'm thinking that, I'm already climbing the stairs, moving to the bedroom that Hudson and I share, seeing the door to the bathroom securely closed, hearing the water running on the other side.

I hesitate, but only for a heartbeat.

Because this is so much more important than a photograph.

I cross the room, turn the handle—relief flowing through me when I find the door unlocked—and push into the bathroom.

He's there, naked and beautiful...and sad, hands braced against the wall, head hanging, shoulders hunched.

Fuck.

I close my eyes for a second, allow the guilt to ripple through me.

I deserve that.

Then I tuck it away.

Because I'm going to make this better. For both of us.

Quietly, I shut the door then strip off my clothes, slowly tugging the plate glass panel open and slipping into the shower behind Hudson.

I know he likely feels the gust of cool air, but he doesn't turn around.

I don't let that dissuade me, just step forward, glad of the waterproof bandage secured over my eyebrow when the water splatters over my face and hair and shoulders. He stiffens when I wrap my arms around his middle, but I don't let that dissuade me either.

Instead, I hug him tightly, pressing my cheek against his back.

Holding the strength of him close.

Giving him some of my own.

"It's not just about what happened today," I murmur, knowing he can hear me when he goes even more stiff. "It's about Colt too." I wait and when he doesn't speak, I go on, "I should have told you what I was thinking. Same as he should have talked to you about taking another tour."

His lungs inflate on a shaky breath.

"I don't know Colt's reasons for keeping that from you, and I hate that you bear the scars of his loss, that those scars are so deep they'll never fully heal."

"Princess—"

"I messed up today," I go on, hugging him more tightly. "And I'm really sorry. I wasn't thinking—and I know that's not an excuse. I seriously believed I could slip in and out and no one would be the wiser." His lungs inflate again. "I get that it was really freaking stupid. You would have come with me, I know you would have. I just..."

"You wanted your dad's picture." He slowly spins in my embrace, and I hold my breath as I shore up my courage to glance up at his face.

He's really mad.

I *really* hurt him.

But when my gaze locks with his, when I stare into the beautiful hazel depths of his eyes, I don't see the hurt or anger.

"I'm sorry," I whisper. "When Dylan surprised me, I realized that my dad would never want me risking my life for a picture, realized how idiotic it was for me to have gone to the house." I settle one hand over his heart. "And I know you wouldn't want that either, that you'd have done anything to stand between me and the person who was trying to hurt me." My fingers flex at the flare of emotions cascading across his face, but I have to finish this. I have to make sure that he understands. "I've done a lot of things in my life—both dumb and smart—and I've had so many wonderful opportunities, and I know that I'm incredibly lucky even despite what's happened over the last couple of years—"

He opens his mouth, but I gently press a finger to his lips, stifling his protest.

"But I know that I'm even luckier...because the universe brought me you."

His eyes shimmer with tears, and I'm not doing any better.

"You're more important than a picture, of course you are. And so is what we're building. I'm sorry I went there and messed up so catastrophically that I risked myself and our future, but I'm even more sorry I let you think for a second that you aren't the beautiful gift you are."

"Princess," he murmurs.

"I know I don't have to ask your permission, and I was a giant jerk for saying that." My throat is tight, but I push out the next words. Because he needs to know. Because he deserves them and so much more. "You've given me freedom and love, understanding and kindness, and I know that I'll need to work to rebuild the trust I broke, but I promise you that I'll do whatever it takes to get there." I take a breath. "I'll share my location. I'll take your advice on making sure I'm safe. I'll even carry a stun gun or take self-defense—"

I don't finish.

Because he's brushing my hand away from his mouth, bending, and slanting his lips over mine.

Kissing me so deeply, so intensely, that my chest is heaving by the time he lifts his head.

And when he does that—even though I want him to keep on kissing me like that for eternity—relief pours through me.

Because he's smiling.

Because his hazel eyes are gentle and filled with love instead of hurt.

And teasing, I realize a moment later.

"I saw what you did to him with that frame, baby," he says, mouth curving as he lightly smooths a hand down my back. "I don't think you need to worry about the self-defense classes."

Laughter bubbles up in my chest.

But I hold it back.

I touch his cheek. "I'm serious, honey."

He covers my hands with his own. "I know." He brushes his lips lightly over my bandage. "And thank you for saying that. I... I know that my instinct to protect may be a little overbearing sometimes, so I don't want you to hesitate to call me out on that, okay?"

I nod.

"And let's talk to Ty. He can be a neutral party and come

up with a plan to make sure you're taking proper precautions... he'll make sure that I don't take my protection detail too far." He touches the backs of his knuckles to my cheek. "Because I know that I'm not always going to be rational when it comes to keeping you safe."

God, is it possible to love this man any more?

I don't think so.

"Honey," I whisper, heart thudding against my ribs.

"I won't ever cage you, princess." A beat. "I promise."

"I know," I tell him, love filling me to bursting. "Because you're the first person to ever help me soar."

EPILOGUE

Dash, *A Year Later...*

"CUT!" The director is on a tear today, and I hate watching her yell at Willow.

Well, technically, she's not yelling. She's...directing.

I don't get this part of Willow's job, but she does. And she's happy. Thriving.

It's incredible to watch her in her element.

And this director, Vivian Krause, is the first one to give her a chance with a leading role.

"I'm needed back in wardrobe," she murmurs as she brushes past me. "See you later?"

"I've got to run some errands, but Ty will be here until I get back."

She smiles and nods, attentive but also distracted.

That's okay.

This is her job.

With the trial finally behind us, and all her money woes

gone, it feels good to be at a stage where we're so comfortable with each other that we practically read each other's minds.

The trial was brutal, forcing her to relive the trauma of her past. The worst part—at least to me—was her mother up there. Defending Dylan. It made me sick. Listening to her talk about a wild, troubled teenager who was out of control. And yet, in recounting her misadventures, there was nothing truly over the top. Not enough to justify her subsequent actions.

A little drug use, but let's be honest—it's rare to find a teenager that doesn't dabble, especially a wealthy one in the public eye. She never hurt anyone, never used hard drugs, and it never impacted her work. Yet her mother seemed determined to paint her as some sort of drug-addled villain.

And it pissed me right off.

Apparently, it pissed off the jury too.

Not only did they find Dylan guilty of aggravated assault, he was also ordered to pay her a fuck-ton of money. The forensic accountant is a fucking magician, if you ask me. He dug up almost every penny of Dylan's financial abuse to go along with the physical and emotional.

Dylan had to sell the house and everything he owned to pay for his legal team and get Willow what he owes her.

The best part?

When he gets out of prison in eight or so years? He *still* owes her six figures.

It's great.

We don't need the money, but putting the screws to Dylan will always make me happy.

I proposed right after the trial, at the top of a canyon in Arizona at sunset.

We're having a winter wedding—next January—in Hawaii. The girls are having a field day with the planning, and I'm man enough to admit that it's fun. Mostly. Sometimes. Cake tasting was fun, at the very least.

My phone rings once I'm in my SUV, heading to take my favorite senior client, Martika, to the doctor.

"Hey, Chuck. What's up?"

"Dude, we're gonna need to think about hiring some more help. Business is fucking booming. Three new clients since yesterday."

"Three?" I ask in surprise.

"Yup. One is Martika's grandson—he needs security for a gala he's hosting. A thousand people. So we'll probably need to hire some freelancers for that one."

"Jesus. But still, good news."

He updates me on a few more things before I pull up to Martika's building.

"Listen I just pulled up to Martika's," I say. "So we can talk about expansion at next week's all-hands meeting."

"Well, now that you have a new partner—"

"Gotta run, man. I'll call you later!" I disconnect and get out to greet Martika.

As ALWAYS, any appointment with Martika runs long.

Her doctor tends to be busy, traffic is usually a nightmare, and she always gets me to walk her in when we get home. So she can feed me, give me water, whatever it takes to keep me around a little longer. And I don't mind—she's lonely. Plus, she pays me incredibly well. I can hang out and make her laugh for a while.

She loves hearing updates on the wedding, so I tell her everything I can remember.

Color scheme, menu, and bridesmaid info makes her giggle.

Then she pulls out pictures of her own wedding. Well, her first wedding. From what I understand, there have been four, and she's outlived all the grooms.

It's getting late, though, and I really need to get going.

I've just gotten into my SUV when a text from Willow pops up.

WILLOW: I need you. In my trailer. Hurry!

My blood runs cold, and I probably break a dozen traffic laws getting back to the set, grateful that this part of the movie is being filmed in L.A. They did two weeks on location in Hawaii—which is what convinced her to have the wedding there—but the rest is all local.

Throwing the vehicle into park, I race past the guards, past some startled members of the crew, and even past Vivian, in a panic about what might be happening to Willow.

And where the hell is Ty?!

I throw open the door to Willow's trailer. "Willow! Babe, what's—" I cut off abruptly.

She's buck naked, sprawled across the small daybed provided for her.

And as my eyes rake over her beautiful body, I realize she's... handcuffed.

"Took you long enough," she murmurs, playfully batting her eyelashes.

"I was..." I can't remember where I am and my mouth feels dry.

Not that we don't already have the most incredible sex possible, but this is different. *Special.*

The ultimate show of trust.

"Where's the key?" I ask automatically, safety always of tantamount importance.

She laughs and motions with her head. "Right there. Now come to bed, Hudson."

She doesn't have to ask me twice.

I take a second to lock the door and start ripping my clothes off.

A moment later I'm on top of her, mouths and bodies in perfect sync as we kiss and touch and...bond. That's the best word to describe this because it's so much more than lovemaking.

She knows I love her.

She knows I'll always take care of her.

She knows she's my everything.

But now I also know she trusts me.

Which means so much to me.

"I love you," I breathe against her lips. "So much."

"I love you more," she whispers back.

Our eyes lock, and my world is stupidly perfect.

"Hudson?"

My eyes snap to hers.

"What are you waiting for? An invitation?"

I rumble out a laugh and press my lips to hers.

"You're in a very compromising position to be so sassy."

"Uh huh." Her eyes twinkle. "Let's go, buddy—I have less than an hour at this point."

"Well... you might be a little late."

Atlas

"And then he says"—her voice drops into a rough approximation of my voice and if I wasn't so annoyed at the gorgeous woman making fun of me a-fucking-gain, I'd be impressed at how good she is at that—"I haven't had a hot dog in my mouth since college."

Yup.

Not one of my finer moments.

But I turn into a bumbling dumbass around this woman.

Lily Maxwell is beautiful. And funny. And smart and talented, a country star who's successfully made the transition to full and complete pop star in the last six months.

People sport T-shirts with lyrics from her songs.

Her tour dates sell out in seconds.

Social media shows her on every other video—or maybe that's just my algorithm because I can't seem to scroll away when she comes up on my phone.

Number one singles. Platinum records. A documentary about her song-writing and the aforementioned tour.

All of which has cemented her spot as an A-lister.

And none of which seem to have changed her.

She's still the same vivacious, smart, confident, and yes, it has to be said, beautiful woman with a mischievous streak a mile wide.

"Dude," Banks mutters, slanting his gaze at me, his green eyes dancing with mirth.

I know.

If it was anyone but me who said that shit, I'd be dying of laughter.

Unfortunately, it was me.

And it is me who's on the receiving end of my friends' laughter. Briar, my assistant—or in actuality, the woman who's become my right hand in my business—cackles the loudest of them all.

And Aspen and Banks, Royal and Jade, Willow and Dash all laugh pretty fucking loudly.

I scowl, lift my glass to my lips, tossing back the dredges of my Gamebreaker, the drink our deceased friend, Colt, created way back in our college years.

No, it doesn't pair well with hot dogs.

Probably why I hadn't had one between then and the last concert of Lily's I attended.

I was starving, the spread was there, and...

So was the infamous Lily Maxwell to overhear my idiocy.

To the rest of the world, I'm Atlas Delarosa, powerful businessman, billionaire before I turned thirty.

To this crew, Lily included, I'm just Atlas—a former college hockey player who is loyal and steadfast and...

Great.

I sound like a golden retriever.

Lily's phone buzzes and, thank fuck, it cuts off the rest of her teasing.

"Excuse me," she says softly, pushing back her chair and striding for the privacy of the hallway of The Sapphire Room.

It's the club my friends and I own, one we started to honor Colt, and now a place that has become a second home for us.

My eyes linger on the entrance to the hall for long enough that Dash kicks my foot.

Hard.

"Dude," he mutters, "you need to pull it together."

"Seriously," Royal says, "you're giving whipped a bad name."

"Pot meet kettle." My words are terse, filled with warning.

One they all ignore.

Because they're my friends. But they're also my family.

And because our love language is giving each other shit.

I ignore Banks when he says, "You need to ask her out."

And Briar when she says, "Exactly. He needs to shit or get off the pot."

"Maybe we should all give Atlas a break," Jade, the nicest of us, murmurs.

"Or maybe he needs a push," Willow, who's also nice, but whose wicked streak comes out more frequently now that Dash and her have fallen in love. "I know I did."

"I need another drink," I growl, shoving up to my feet and striding to the bar, trying very hard to keep my gaze away from that empty hallway where Lily disappeared.

It's just...

She's taken a lot of phone calls tonight.

Like an obscene amount—and that's saying something, considering my cell is perpetually glued to my ear.

That's why I leave my empty glass on the bar, turn for the hall.

Her voice reaches me before I see her.

"...I'm not trying to be dramatic Erin, but that's not going to work for me."

I frown, move a little closer, drifting through the corridor and toward the woman standing near to the door to the parking lot, phone to her ear, chin to her chest, tension wound tightly through every inch of her frame.

My frown deepens.

Because this isn't the Lily I've come to know over the last months.

She's light and joy, mirth and mischief...not this picture of frustration with a hint of gloominess.

As if the weight she's carrying is heavy.

Too heavy.

When every interaction I've had with her before now makes it seem as if worldwide stardom has barely touched her.

I step closer and she starts, head jerking up, eyes going wide for a heartbeat before I see it.

A mask slipping back into place.

She smiles at me, tosses her hair—bright and bubbly slipping back into place. "Just take care of it Erin, yeah? Within the next couple of hours."

Then she's tapping at her phone's screen, letting her hand with it held tight in its grasp fall to her side. "Easy on the scowling, big guy," she says lightly, her smile widening. "Otherwise your face may stay like that."

"I—"

That's so far from what I was expecting her to say that I fumble for a second.

Hell, who am I kidding?

I'm always fumbling over myself with this woman.

Stammering. Dropping shit. Running into things.

It's so beyond fucking pathetic that I almost let her slip by me. Except...she has a problem.

And if there's anything I'm good at, it's fixing things.

I catch her arm as she starts to brush by me. "What's wrong?"

A tug, trying to free herself from my grip. But I can't seem to let her go.

"What does Erin need to fix?"

Her brows drag together and I want to kiss the befuddlement off her face.

But...something to fix, some way for me to stop feeling like an idiot with this woman.

"Lily," I warn.

She jerks slightly, her startling blue eyes locking on mine, and she doesn't fight me for once, just says, "My charter to Denver fell through. I'm supposed to leave tonight for the next leg of my tour, and my assistant has supposedly looked into every option...and landed with me taking a commercial flight."

My eyebrows fly up.

"I'm not trying to be a diva," she says quietly.

"You being on a commercial flight right now is stupid," I mutter. "At best you'll be mobbed. At worst things could get scary quickly."

She nibbles at her red-painted lips. "I know." A shrug then I watch the worry being wiped clear of her face. "It'll be fine. Erin will take care of it."

"Come with me," I blurt.

Confusion in blue eyes. "Um...where are we going, big guy?"

"I can give you a ride on my private jet," I say in a rush. "I was heading to Denver tomorrow, anyway." A lie, but not a huge one. I need to check in with the office there. It just wasn't at the top of my priority list.

"You were?" Her brow furrows.

"I have an office there."

Her face relaxes. "I can't ask you to—"

"It's not asking. I'm offering. I have a jet, Lily." I glance at my watch. "I'll make call, have it ready by ten. Does that give you enough time?"

"Atlas," she begins, and the protest hasn't left her tone.

"It's heading that direction," I say, grasping at straws, unable to let this go. "God knows the environment would prefer if someone more than me was on it."

"So, you're saying we should carpool to minimize our carbon footprint?"

Well now, that sounds dumb.

And...I turn back into an idiot.

"I—um... Well— I just—"

Then I catch it—humor in blue eyes, red lips curving into a hint of a smile.

The damned woman is teasing me. Again.

"Lily," I warn again.

A flicker of something through her face—heat maybe? But

before I can really process it, her voice is gentling. "Thank you, Atlas." She lifts on tiptoe, presses her lips to my cheek. "I really appreciate the offer. I'll see you at ten."

My skin burns from the contact, from the agreement.

Then she's slipping her arm free of my grip and I know that nothing is going to stay the same.

Because I'm not going to let it.

We hope you loved DEALBREAKER as much as we loved writing Willow and Dash's story! If you want to find out how our favorite broody billionaire falls, don't miss RULE-BREAKER! **She's everything I shouldn't want. But that's never stopped me before...**

CLICK HERE TO READ RULEBREAKER NOW>

GAMEBREAKERS

Icebreaker
Heartbreaker
Dealbreaker
Rulebreaker
Oathbreaker

ABOUT THE AUTHORS

USA Today bestselling author, Elise Faber, loves chocolate, Star Wars, Harry Potter, and hockey (the order depending on the day and how well her team — the Sharks! — are playing). She and her husband also play as much hockey as they can squeeze into their schedules, so much so that their typical date night is spent on the ice. Elise is the mom to two exuberant boys and lives in Northern California. Connect with her in her Facebook group, the Fabinators or find more information about her books at www.elisefaber.com.

facebook.com/elisefaberauthor
amazon.com/author/elisefaber
bookbub.com/profile/elise-faber
instagram.com/elisefaber
tiktok.com/@elisefaberauthor
goodreads.com/elisefaber
patreon.com/EliseFaber

ABOUT THE AUTHORS

USA Today Bestselling author Kat Mizera was born in Miami Beach with a healthy dose of wanderlust. She's lived from coast to coast, and everywhere in between, but home is wherever her family is.

A devoted mom and wife to her wonderful and supportive husband (Kevin) and two amazing boys (Nick and Max), Kat loves to travel the globe with her adventurous, hockey loving family. Greece is at the top of that list. She hopes to one day retire there, spending her days writing books on the beach.

Kat is former freelance sports writer who now writes steamy hockey romance about her favorite fictional teams, the Las Vegas Sidewinders and the Alaska Blizzard. The library of novels she's penned also include sexy contemporary stories about baseball stars, alpha sex club owners, special forces heroes, rock stars and royalty. Regardless of genre, her books about bad boys with hearts of gold will steal your breath, rock your world and melt your heart.

WHERE TO FOLLOW KAT:

www.katmizera.com

Kat's Private Facebook Group

https://bit.ly/KatMizeraFBGroup

facebook.com/authorkatmizera

instagram.com/katmizera

www.ingramcontent.com/pod-product-compliance
Lightning Source LLC
LaVergne TN
LVHW012340100826
845148LV00018B/2867

9781637491478